"All right, Kate," Annie said. "We've outlined our dramas, so spill it. What is Kate Morgan dealing with right now?"

Kate shook her head. "I feel a little weird because for once there isn't any drama in my life," she said.

"Well, don't worry," Cooper told Kate. "Things might seem okay now, but something is bound to happen. It always does."

"What a cheerful thought," Kate said. "Can we get back to having a good time now?"

Cooper and Annie laughed at the serious face she was making. "Fine," Cooper said. "But when whatever it is that's going to happen happens, don't forget we told you so."

"How could I?" asked Kate. "You'd never let me."

Follow the Circle:

circle of three

BOOK 13

and it harm none

isobel Bird

AVON BOOKS

An Imprint of HarperCollinsPublishers

And It Harm None

Copyright © 2002 by Isobel Bird

All rights reserved. No part of this book may be used or
reproduced in any manner whatsoever without written
permission except in the case of brief quotations embodied
in critical articles or reviews.
Printed in the United States of America.
For information address HarperCollins Children's Books,
a division of HarperCollins Publishers,
1350 Avenue of the Americas,
New York, NY 10019.

Library of Congress Catalog Card Number: 2001118053
ISBN 0-06-000605-6

First Avon edition, 2002

❖

AVON TRADEMARK REG. U.S. PAT. OFF. AND IN OTHER COUNTRIES,
MARCA REGISTRADA, HECHO EN U.S.A.

Visit us on the World Wide Web!
www.harperteen.com

circle of three

and it harm none

CHAPTER 1

"Good Goddess," Cooper exclaimed. "Was it this cold last year?"

She was standing at the edge of the water in the cove at Ryder Beach. The waves washed gently over her bare feet, wetting the hem of the white robe she was wearing.

"It was colder," answered Kate from behind her. Kate was attempting to start a fire in the circle of stones they had just finished making, and the matches were giving her a hard time. The wind wasn't helping, either. Every time she got a match lit a little breath of air would come along and blow it out again. It was as if the wind was teasing her, and it was becoming annoying.

Annie was having better luck with the candles. Those at least were in glass holders, which made things easier. It also made it easier to stick them in the sand, forming a larger ring around the makeshift fire pit.

Soon Kate was encircled by a ring of flickering light.

"Finally," she said as she struck yet another match and held it to the newspaper she was using as kindling. This time the flame held, and soon the paper was crackling away. Shortly thereafter the driftwood that formed a pyramid over the paper caught fire as well.

Cooper dipped the bowl in her hands into the waves and let the water fill it. She carried it back to the circle and set it near the fire. Another bowl already sat there, filled with salt, and a bundle of white sage leaves tied with red string lay beside it.

"I think that's everything," said Cooper. "Are you witchlets ready to get this party started?"

"By all means," Kate said.

"Let's do it," added Annie.

The three of them stood around the fire Kate had started, looking at one another happily. Above them a perfectly round, full moon gazed on as they began their ritual.

Cooper picked up the bowl of salt. Taking a pinch in her fingers, she walked clockwise around the circle of candles, sprinkling the salt behind her as she went.

"With the power of earth I cast a circle," she intoned. "May it be as strong as the mountains and as fertile as a garden."

She returned to the center of the circle and placed the bowl of salt back on the ground. Then

Annie picked up the bundle of sage. She held it to the fire's flames until it began to smoke. Then she walked around the circle, just as Cooper had done. The smoke filled the air with its pungent scent as Annie waved the sage gently from side to side.

"With the power of air I cast a circle," she said. "May it be as wild as the wind and as loving as a whisper."

When she returned and placed the still-burning sage beside the bowl of salt, it was Kate's turn to strengthen the circle. She took a piece of driftwood that she'd set aside and lit it in the fire. As she carried it around the circle she said, "With the power of fire I cast a circle. May it be as fierce as a wildfire and as warming as the sun."

When she had come back to the others, Cooper picked up the bowl of seawater. They each dipped their hands into it, cupping some of the water in their fingers. Then they each turned to face outward in a different direction.

"With the power of water we cast a circle," Cooper said, sprinkling the water around her area of the circle.

"May it be as mysterious as the ocean," Annie continued as she spread the water in her hands over the sand in front of her.

"And as healing as rain," Kate added, completing the circle by sprinkling the ground around her.

The three friends turned to face one another once more.

"The circle is cast," said Annie.

"We are between the worlds," Kate said.

"And we are *very* chilly," added Cooper solemnly.

The three of them cracked up. "I don't think that's part of any circle-casting ritual I've ever read," said Kate admonishingly.

"Hey," Cooper said. "It's all about being spontaneous, right? There's no right or wrong way to do this stuff."

The three of them knelt in the sand around the fire, making themselves comfortable. Annie picked up the bundle of sage leaves and tossed it into the flames, where it burned slowly, emitting clouds of smoke.

"That was a nice addition," commented Kate.

"I picked it up at the bookstore," explained Annie. "Sage is good for cleansing sacred space. Dixie used it in the ritual we did at my old house," she added, referring to a Wiccan friend who had helped her try to send the ghosts of her parents through the veil when Annie had mistakenly believed that they were angry with her.

"Now we're all cleansed and cast and sitting here in sacred space. Can you guys believe we've been doing this for a year now?" Kate asked.

"Yes and no," Annie replied. "It seems like just yesterday that you came and asked me why I had checked out that book of spells."

It had, in fact, been almost a year since Kate had discovered *Spells and Charms for the Modern*

Witch in the school library while doing research for a history class assignment. That was the book that had started it all. First Kate had done the Come to Me Love Spell, with disastrous results. Then she'd enlisted first Annie and then Cooper— who had both previously checked out the same book—to help her fix her mistake. They'd made an even bigger mess of things, and ultimately they'd been forced to ask for assistance from some local witches before things were finally straightened out.

Now the three girls had gathered at the cove to celebrate a year of friendship and magical work. It had been at the same cove that they'd done their first serious ritual. Since that night they'd done many rituals together. In that time all of their lives had changed in ways they could never have expected, and they were far different people from the ones who had sat there the February before.

Now they sat looking into the flames of the ritual fire. At that first ritual they had each given up to the fire something that they wanted to free themselves from before then asking for certain things to be brought into their lives. For their anniversary ritual they had decided that they would once again give things up to the fire. Only this time the things they gave would be offerings of thanks for everything that had happened to them. They had learned that one of the principles of magic was that you should always remember to thank the universe for helping you achieve your intentions.

All three of them had brought their gifts with them, but they hadn't discussed with each other what those gifts were. Now they took them out and held them in their hands.

"Who wants to go first?" Kate asked.

"I will," said Annie. She looked into the fire and paused as she thought back to the night a year before. "My wish last year was that I not worry so much," she said. Then she laughed gently. "I'm not sure I worry *all* that much less, but I do know that I'm a lot more confident now than I was then. And the things I have to worry about now are so much more interesting than they were then," she added.

She looked at the gift in her hands. It was a small painting she'd done, a watercolor on paper. It depicted her dancing beneath the moon, her arms stretched out and her head thrown back.

"I feel a lot freer because of what's happened to me this year," she said as she held the picture to the flames and watched it begin to burn. "I was able to finally say good-bye to my parents, and even that little disaster with aspecting Freya last summer had some good parts to it. I also feel very lucky to have friends like you guys and a community like the one we're part of." The paper was burning swiftly, and Annie dropped it into the heart of the fire, where it blackened and curled.

They waited a moment, watching her gift turn

to ash and smoke that soared up from the fire pit. Then Kate said, "My turn."

She held up a small cake. "I baked this," she said. "It's an almond cake. I read in some book that people used to leave almond cakes as gifts for the Goddess in some cultures."

She crumbled the cake into the flames, where the bits and pieces blackened. Kate watched them burn.

"Last year I wished that I could not be so afraid of change," she said. She sighed. "Well, I certainly had a lot of chances to work on *that* this year. I'm not sure how I did, but I think I learned a lot. Between Aunt Netty's cancer, breaking up with Tyler, and coming out of the broom closet to my parents, I had enough change to last me for quite a while." She looked at Cooper and Annie. "Not that I believe for a second that there won't be even more changes coming up," she finished as they all laughed.

It was Cooper's turn, and she held out a piece of notebook paper. "I wrote a song," she said. "It's about how I've changed this year because of being involved in witchcraft. I'm not going to read it to you," she added, "and this is the only copy of it. Once it's gone, it's gone. I want it to be a real gift, something I'm giving back without keeping any of it for myself."

She consigned the song to the fire, watching it smoke and burn.

"Last year I wished that I could give people more of a chance," she said. "I think I've been able to do that, at least a little. I gave T.J. a chance, and it turned out to be really great. I met Jane, and I'm really thankful for that. And I gave Wicca a chance," she added. "That was the most important thing." She looked at Kate and Annie. "I mean besides being friends with you guys, of course," she said, grinning.

The three of them sat around the fire for a while in silence, watching it burn. The waves lapped gently on the beach and the sea air blew over their faces. Then Annie began to sing, quietly. "We all come from the Goddess, and to her we shall return."

"Like a drop of rain," Cooper and Kate joined in, "flowing to the ocean."

They sang the song through, their voices blending together. Cooper's was the strongest, confident and self-assured; Annie's was pleasant and soft; and Kate's was determined, if a little off-key. They sang happily and unself-consciously, the words rising with the flames and the smoke from the fire. Then, as if by unspoken agreement, they stood and joined hands. Circling the fire, they did a slow dance, raising and lowering their clasped hands as they continued to sing. Their voices spiraled up, wrapping around one another and soaring toward the moon.

"We all come from the Goddess, and to her we

shall return like a drop of rain, flowing to the ocean." The simple song captured the moment perfectly with its message of renewal and celebration. The girls had sung it at numerous rituals throughout the year, but now it belonged entirely to them, and to the moment. It was as if they were the only ones who had ever sung it.

When the song finished, they stopped dancing and stood still. The girls looked at one another, still holding hands. Annie squeezed Cooper's hand and said, "Blessed be." Cooper then did the same to Kate, who in turn gave Annie the traditional witches' greeting. Then all three of them joined together in saying, "Merry meet, and merry part, and merry meet again. The circle is open but unbroken."

With that the ritual was over, at least the official part. There was still more, but it had to wait until they had dismantled the circle, removed their robes, and put away all of their magical items in the backpacks they'd carried with them. Then the three of them left the cove, walking across the beach to the stairs that led to the wharf.

They trudged up the steps and walked to Cooper's car, where they put their stuff in the back. Then they went to the Frozen Moo, their favorite ice cream shop, where they commandeered a booth at the back and ordered hot fudge sundaes all around. When the ice cream came, Cooper held up her spoon.

"A toast," she said. "To surviving a year of friendship."

"That's not exactly positive, is it?" Kate said. "You make it sound like an ordeal."

Cooper looked thoughtful. "I think it was more like boot camp," she said.

"Oh, that's *much* better," Annie teased. She held up her own spoon. "How about to a year of living magically?"

Kate groaned. "That's so New Agey," she complained.

"Let's see you come up with something, then," said Cooper.

Kate hoisted her spoon. "To a year on the path," she said, looking at her friends for approval.

Annie and Cooper nodded. "That will do," said Cooper.

The girls clinked their spoons together and then plunged them into their sundaes. They each took a big bite of ice cream and hot fudge and savored the taste.

"This is how all rituals should end," remarked Annie.

"Let's suggest it in class next week," Cooper replied.

"Do you guys realize there are only a few more weeks until the initiation ceremony?" asked Kate, licking her spoon.

Annie nodded. "I know," she said. "I'm getting

a little nervous. I'm not sure I know enough to make this decision."

"Come on," Cooper said, giving her friend a look. "It's not like this is a chemistry test. You don't have to study for it or anything."

"I know," Annie responded. "But it's a big deal. I just want to make sure I'm doing the right thing."

"What do you think happens at the ceremony?" Kate said.

The others were quiet, clearly thinking about the possibilities. The truth was, they had no way of knowing. The initiation ceremony was a secret, and no one who had gone through it would tell them anything. "Besides," Archer had told them, "it changes every year."

That didn't stop the girls from thinking about what might be in store for them should they decide to go through with the ceremony. But they rarely discussed it among themselves. This was the first time any of them had actually brought it up for debate.

"I have so many other things to worry about right now," said Annie. "That's sort of the last thing I can think about."

"Have your aunt and Grayson made any decisions about moving yet?" asked Cooper.

Annie's Aunt Sarah was getting married shortly before the initiation ceremony, and a decision had to be made about whether the family would remain in Beecher Falls or move to San Francisco, where Grayson Dunning and his daughter, Becka, lived in the Crandalls' old house. Annie and her friends hoped that the couple would choose to remain in Beecher Falls, but this was something else they rarely talked about openly because none of them could bear thinking about her leaving.

"No," Annie said shortly. "They haven't made up their minds. Becka and I have stopped talking about it because it just makes us stress out. I'm trying to concentrate on only positive things, like Juliet."

"How is your big sis anyway?" Kate inquired.

Juliet was Juliet Garrison. A few weeks before, Annie had discovered that her mother had once had a child and that she'd given it up for adoption. After contacting an adoption search service, she'd received a call from Juliet. The two had talked, and after exchanging information had determined that Juliet was, in fact, Annie's older sister.

Annie was still adjusting to the idea of having a big sister. While she was excited, there were still some issues, namely that she hadn't told Aunt Sarah that she'd found Juliet. Her aunt, who had been the one to tell Annie about the adopted baby, didn't know that her niece had taken things a step further. Neither did Annie's little sister, Meg, who didn't even know about their missing sister. Annie was trying to decide how to tell them about locating Juliet, and she hadn't figured out yet what she should do.

"She's great," Annie said, answering Kate's question. "We've talked a few times now. I really like her. But I'm not sure what happens next." She sighed deeply. "This is a big deal."

"You'll figure it out," Cooper said reassuringly. "You always do."

Annie nodded. "I hope so," she said. "There's so much going on that I feel like this would be like dropping a bomb on an unsuspecting village. But enough about that. How's your mother doing?"

This question was addressed to Cooper. Her mother had, in the past month, begun drinking more than was good for her. Cooper knew it was a result of the stress she was under because of the divorce from Cooper's father, but that didn't make it any easier to take. Cooper had briefly moved out of the house to give herself some time to think, living with her friend Sasha and Sasha's adoptive mother, Thea—a member of a local coven—for a while. She'd moved back into the house since then, mainly because her father had asked her to. He was worried about her mother, he said, and felt better with Cooper in the house to keep an eye on her.

Since then her mother's behavior hadn't gotten any worse—but it hadn't gotten any better, either. She spent most of her time in her room. When Cooper did see her, she was sullen and uncommunicative. Several times Cooper had tried to discuss the situation with her, but each time her mother had simply gone into her bedroom and shut the door.

"She's the same," Cooper told her friends. "I don't know what's going to happen. Right now I think she's keeping things at least a little under control because she has to teach. But once school is out for the summer, I don't know what will happen."

Annie put an arm around Cooper and silently leaned her head against Cooper's for a second. Then she let go. "All right, Kate," she said. "We've outlined our dramas, so spill it. What is Kate Morgan dealing with right now?"

Kate shook her head. "I feel a little weird because for once there isn't any drama in my life," she said. *Not that there wasn't last month*, she thought to herself. Although her friends didn't know about it, she'd just recently stopped going to the therapist her parents had sent her to after discovering her involvement in Wicca. Kate had never told Cooper and Annie about that. She didn't know why, really, except that having a therapist had embarrassed her. But now it was over. And so was her relationship with Tyler. Another secret her friends didn't know was that Tyler had asked her to get back together.

"Well, don't worry," Cooper told Kate. "Things might seem okay now, but something is bound to happen. It always does."

"What a cheerful thought," Kate said. "Can we get back to having a good time now?"

Cooper and Annie laughed at the serious face

she was making. "Fine," Cooper said. "But when whatever it is that's going to happen happens, don't forget we told you so."

"How could I?" asked Kate. "You'd never let me."

CHAPTER 2

"Can you even believe the lame theme they came up with for the dance this year?"

Tara, who had just voiced the question, took a bite of her sandwich and rolled her eyes. Jessica, sitting across from her, nibbled on a carrot stick, pushed her long blond hair behind one ear, and nodded in agreement. "Very tired," she said.

Kate contemplated the salad she'd brought for lunch. I think I put too much dressing on it, she thought critically as she licked her lips and tasted honey mustard. She'd been spending a lot of time helping her mother with her catering business, and as a result she frequently found herself rating the various items she consumed. It was, she thought, becoming something of a problem.

"I mean, hasn't the whole famous lovers thing been done about a billion times?" Tara continued.

"Two billion," Jessica said. "Our masquerade ball idea last year was *so* much better."

As Kate listened to her friends talk she couldn't

help but think back to the previous year's Valentine's Day dance. That's when everything had started. She and her friends had been responsible for coming up with a theme for the dance. More important, she had been just the tiniest bit obsessed with getting hunky football player Scott Coogan to ask her to the dance. That's when she'd done the spell—the spell that had backfired so badly and gotten her in all that trouble.

Things certainly had changed since then. Scott was gone, off at college somewhere and out of Kate's life. She, Annie, and Cooper were best friends. Tara and Jessica, two of her former best friends, were back in her life after an awkward and painful falling out. And Sherrie, the remaining member of their once-solid quartet, was now on the outs with everyone. That last fact made Kate particularly happy. Sherrie Adams was trouble with a capital *T*, and the less Kate had to deal with her, the better.

"What do you think, Kate?" Tara asked. "Want to run for queen again this year?"

Kate looked up and saw her friends grinning at her. They knew that the whole issue of the Valentine's dance queen and king was a sore spot with her. One of the results of her misdirected spell the year before had been that practically every boy in school had nominated her for queen. It had enraged all the other girls, and Kate had found herself ostracized by her friends and even competing against Tara, who had been put forth as a candidate by the basketball team. At the time, her friends had had no idea that Kate's sudden popularity was the result of magic gone wrong. Now that they did, they liked to tease her about it.

"Sure," Jessica said. "Maybe this year you could do a spell to make all the other contestants' hair fall out."

Kate narrowed her eyes. "Or maybe I could just make sure *you* get nominated this year," she said. She knew the idea of running for Valentine's Day queen was shy Jessica's worst nightmare. Sure enough, her friend paled at the suggestion.

"I'm not even *going* to the dance," Jessica said testily.

"Me neither," Tara added. "It just doesn't seem all that much fun this year."

Kate nodded in agreement with her friends. "The only person with a boyfriend is Cooper, and you know she won't go," she joked.

"We should just throw our own dateless Valentine's Day party," Jessica remarked as she picked up another carrot stick.

Kate looked at her two friends. "Why not?" she said.

"Why not what?" asked Tara, scratching her nose.

"Why not have our own Valentine's Day party?" said Kate. "It would be fun. We could all go out to dinner and then do something we want to do instead of standing around at a stupid dance."

"Okay," said Jessica. "It sounds good to me."

"Yeah," Tara said after a moment. "It does. Count me in."

"Great," Kate said, suddenly feeling excited about having a project. "I'll talk to Cooper and Annie and see what they think. But I'm sure it will be a go."

The bell signaling the end of the period rang and the girls gathered up their stuff and left. As she walked to her next class, Kate was happy. For the first time in a long while, things seemed to be going smoothly. She was getting along with her family and her friends. She was enjoying the Wicca study group. She had a fun project to look forward to. Everything was fine.

Her good spirits held up all through Mr. Niemark's math class, despite the fact that they had a surprise quiz. Totally by accident, Kate had actually read the material they were being tested on, and she did well on the quiz. When that period was over she walked confidently into Ms. Ableman's science class feeling like nothing could possibly spoil her mood.

Not even Sherrie, although the two of them hadn't spoken a word to each other all year, and most of the time Kate didn't even think about the fact that they sat only a few rows away from one another in science class. As she took her seat, Kate looked at the back of Sherrie's head and wondered what her former friend would think if she knew that Kate and the others were planning their own Valentine's Day get-together. In the past, Sherrie would have been right in the middle of things. Now she might as well be a total stranger, and that's just how Kate wanted it.

Ms. Ableman came in and stood behind her desk at the front of the room. She looked out at the class, taking mental note of who was absent, and then made some marks in the attendance book in front of her.

"All right," she said, shutting the book. "Well, as I'm sure you all know, the middle of the semester is almost here again. That means we have another big test coming up."

There was a collective groan from the class. Ms. Ableman's tests were legendary at Beecher Falls High School. They always involved some elaborate project or experiment, and they also counted for half of a student's grade in the course. Kate had done fairly well on the previous exam, and she was pretty sure she could pull it off again. Still, the thought of having to prepare for another test dampened her spirits, if only slightly.

"I know not all of you are looking forward to this," said Ms. Ableman, smiling slightly as some of the students laughed. "That's why I've decided to try something a little different."

Kate perked up. Something different? What did Ms. Ableman have in mind, she wondered. Maybe it would be something interesting. Suddenly the idea of a test didn't sound quite as bad as it had moments before.

"Your exam will consist of a practical and a written report," said the teacher.

That's not so bad, Kate thought.

"And you're going to work in teams," the teacher continued. "Your team will be graded as a unit, meaning that you will both receive the same grade."

Kate liked that idea. Working with someone else would mean she had to do only half of the work. *As long as you pick someone good,* she reminded herself. She started scanning the room, thinking about who she could ask to be her teammate. She'd narrowed her choice down to Bob Hines or Jessica Brand when Ms. Ableman said, "I have taken the liberty of choosing your partners for you."

Kate's attention snapped to the front of the room. Ms. Ableman had already selected their partners? That hardly seemed fair. For a moment she panicked. *Calm down,* she told herself reassuringly. *You could still get Bob or Jessica.* When she thought about it, Kate realized that pretty much anyone would be fine as a partner. After all, they were doing a practical and writing about their findings. That wouldn't be hard at all. She was good about keeping detailed notes, and writing them up would be easy. *You've as good as got an A,* she told herself.

Ms. Ableman removed a piece of paper from her desk. "Here are your partners," she said. "Vicki Harper, you'll be working with Martin Beemer. Paul Tarrip, you're paired with Alex Golden." She went down the list, matching up students. Kate waited for her name to be called. Finally, it was.

"Kate Morgan," said Ms. Ableman, nodding at Kate, "you'll be working with Sherrie Adams."

Kate's heart seemed to stop in her chest. Had she heard correctly? Had Ms. Ableman just said what she thought she'd said? She was working with *Sherrie*? No, it wasn't possible. There were twenty other students she could be paired with. It just couldn't be Sherrie.

Ms. Ableman was reading out more names, oblivious to the fact that she had just done the one thing in the world that could make Kate's day fall completely apart. As Kate listened, she wanted more than anything to raise her hand and ask to be reassigned. But how could she do that without making a scene? Everyone would know that she didn't want to work with Sherrie. Sherrie herself would already know, of course. Kate stared at her, wondering what she was thinking. Was she as horrified by the prospect of their working together as Kate was? *How could she not be?* Kate thought. Surely having to talk to Kate, let alone work together on a project that was going to be half of their grade, was enough to push Sherrie over the edge. But at the moment Sherrie was simply staring out the windows that lined one side of the room.

When Ms. Ableman finished reading the list of teams, she picked up another stack of papers. "These are your project assignments," she said.

"Each team has a different one, so there won't be any temptation for teams to *share* their results with one another. Now, I want you to pair up with your teammate, come get your assignment, and spend the rest of the period looking it over."

All around her, other students stood up and went to talk to their partners. Kate found that she just could not force her legs to move. She sat in her chair, looking at Sherrie, who also didn't make any move to come talk to her. Finally, Kate willed herself to stand.

You can do this, she told herself. *You can do it.*

Reluctantly, she walked over to where Sherrie was sitting. "I guess we're partners," she said neutrally.

Sherrie looked at her, an expression of deepest disgust on her face.

"I don't like this any more than you do," Kate said. "Let's just get it over with."

Sherrie stood and together they walked over to Ms. Ableman's desk. The teacher handed Kate their assignment and the two of them went to a table to look it over. Kate read the sheet first while Sherrie sat silently, sullenly picking at her cuticles. "Well?" she said finally.

"We have to do an experiment with plants," Kate said. "We're going to grow them in different conditions and report on what happens."

"Plants?" Sherrie said, sounding as if she'd just discovered something really nasty on the bottom of her shoe. "I have to work with *plants?*"

"It's just seedlings, really," Kate said. "They're not going to get all that big in two weeks."

Sherrie snorted. "This is just perfect," she said. "First I get stuck with you, and now I have to grow things."

"I'm no happier about this than you are," snapped Kate. "But this project is important, and I'm not going to get a bad grade. So why don't you just lose the attitude?"

Sherrie glared at her. "Don't be bossing me around," she said.

"Don't give me a reason to," replied Kate. She'd already decided that she wasn't going to put up with any of Sherrie's games. "Now, let's read over this assignment and decide who's going to do what."

They spent the rest of the period planning their project. Kate was relieved when the bell rang and she could get away from Sherrie. She was even more relieved that her next period was gym. Because she was on the basketball team, she got to spend the period practicing with the other girls who also played on the team. That meant that she, Tara, and Jessica had a chance to hang out and play some ball. As they practiced their shots Kate told them what had happened in Ms. Ableman's class.

"Oh, man," Tara said as she snapped a free throw and it went in. "I wouldn't be you for anything."

"Sherrie doesn't work well with others under

the best of circumstances," said Jessica. "This is going to be a nightmare."

Kate sighed. She'd been trying desperately to convince herself otherwise, but she knew her friends were right. "What am I going to do?" she asked plaintively. "I have got to do well on this."

"Too bad there's not a spell that would make Sherrie tolerable," Tara joked, passing Kate the ball.

Kate caught the ball and ran for the basket. As she jumped up and tipped the ball into the net, she thought about Tara's comment. *Maybe there is a spell*, she thought to herself as she landed on her feet and the ball fell back into her hands.

That afternoon when she got home, Kate went right to her room. Putting her stuff down, she went to her bookcase and looked for a book she'd gotten at Crones' Circle a few months before. It was a book of rituals and spells. She'd glanced through it briefly but hadn't really had a chance to look at it in depth yet. But she recalled a spell that had caught her eye. This is what she was looking for.

She found it on page 153. "A Spell for Neutralizing Hatred," she read. "This spell is useful for eliminating feelings of anger toward someone. It is particularly useful when you need to create a peaceful atmosphere around you." Kate nodded emphatically. "That's *exactly* what I need," she said.

The spell seemed simple enough. All it called for was a black candle. Kate had one of those. She retrieved it from the box of magical items she kept in her closet. Then she sat on the floor in the middle of her room, the book open beside her. She read the directions for the spell, then closed the book. She sat with the candle in her hands and closed her eyes.

The instructions for doing the spell said that she should think about the person she had angry feelings about. She should, it said, think about everything she really hated about this person.

That's easy, Kate thought as she imagined Sherrie's face in her mind. Then she let herself feel every negative feeling she could about her old friend. She thought about all of the horrible things Sherrie had ever said to her or about her. She thought about all of the mean things Sherrie had done to Kate and to her friends. It wasn't difficult; Sherrie had done a lot of things to be angry at her for. In just a few minutes Kate's mind was a tornado of angry thoughts. They swirled around in an ugly, black cloud, making her feel sick with hatred.

The next step of the spell involved imagining the black candle standing in the center of the cloud of angry thoughts. Kate pictured it towering into the sky like a great black pillar. She imagined her anger swirling around it, trying to knock it over and being unable to. She imagined her feelings toward Sherrie as a violent storm tearing across the land.

The candle was in its way, and the storm wanted more than anything to knock it down.

But it couldn't. The candle stood steady as the winds buffeted it and screamed at it. And then the candle began to absorb the blackness. It sucked all of Kate's negativity into itself, filling with the full force of her anger. As the candle took in more and more of her hatred, the tornado became weaker and weaker. It swirled less forcefully, until finally it was nothing but a few gusts of air. Then these, too, were absorbed by the candle and the storm was over.

Kate sat with the candle—now filled with her anger—and imagined herself standing beside it, looking up at the tower where all of her feelings about Sherrie were stored. They were safe inside it. Nobody could let them out except her, and she wasn't going to do that. Instead she was going to light the candle and burn it. As it burned, her negative feelings would be burned away with it. They would be transformed into energy and returned to the universe.

She opened her eyes and looked at the candle in her hands. It looked exactly the same as it had before she did the ritual. But something about it *felt* different. Kate knew that her spell had worked—at least the first part of it had. She'd been able to channel her negative feelings into the candle. She'd worked with energy enough over the past year to sense the subtle change in the way she felt inside. She was more at peace, more confident that she could handle working with Sherrie.

At least I think *I can*, she told herself as she reached for a match.

CHAPTER 3

"Okay," Aunt Sarah said to Annie. "So, what's the big surprise?"

They were sitting across from one another at a fast-food restaurant. Normally, Annie would never set foot in a place that served food in cartons emblazoned with a smiling clown and which employed orange, red, and yellow as its primary decorating colors, but she had particular reasons for wanting to be in a very public place when she made her announcement to her aunt. Being surrounded by loud families and children cramming fries and shakes into their mouths made her feel a little more at ease. Somehow, she thought, it would be harder for Aunt Sarah to yell at her in such surroundings— at least without drawing unwanted attention to herself. She'd suggested that the two of them have dinner and maybe do a little shopping, as Meg was at a friend's house for the evening.

"Well," Annie began tentatively. She chewed her hamburger thoughtfully, briefly wondering what exactly was in the "special sauce" that graced its rubbery surface, and then said, "Well" again.

She paused, totally unclear on how to proceed. She'd gone over and over her speech in her mind, until finally it had seemed to her to be just about perfect. Now, though, sitting and actually facing her aunt, she realized that perhaps it wasn't going to be quite so simple.

"I've been doing a lot of thinking about what you told me," she said finally. "You know, about Mom and the baby," she added when her aunt looked confused.

Aunt Sarah nodded. "Oh," she said. "Right. You know, I'm sorry I told you the way I did. I know it must have seemed really careless."

Annie shook her head. "No," she said. "It's fine. In fact," she continued, "I'm really glad you did."

Aunt Sarah sipped her milk shake and made a face. "Do you know there's no actual milk in these things?" she said to her niece. "They're all chemicals. It's too bad, because they taste great."

"What do you think the baby is like now?" Annie asked suddenly.

Aunt Sarah put down her shake. "I have no idea," she said. "To tell the truth, I hadn't really thought about her until you mentioned what that astrologer told you."

"Would you like to know?" asked Annie, the nervousness in her stomach threatening to erupt at any second as she waited for her aunt's answer.

Aunt Sarah sighed. "I don't know," she said. "It was so long ago, and part of me thinks it's best left in the past." She looked at Annie for a long moment. "Why?" she asked.

Annie swallowed. "That's kind of what the surprise is," she said.

A strange look came over her aunt's face. "What do you mean?" she said.

Annie was wringing her hands under the table. "I sort of found her," she said. As soon as the words were out she felt all of the tension in her body leak out like air from a deflating raft. *There*, she thought, *I said it.*

"You sort of found her," Aunt Sarah repeated slowly. "How much sort of?"

"I did find her," Annie clarified. "I've spoken to her. Several times."

Aunt Sarah had gone white. She sat back in the booth and just stared at Annie for a long time. "How?" she asked finally, her voice barely a whisper.

Annie explained to her aunt how she had found a letter from the agency that had handled the adoption of her sister, and how she'd searched for it on the Internet and come across a site that connected people looking for information about adopted children. "And she called me," Annie concluded.

"I don't believe it," said Aunt Sarah. "I just don't believe it."

She had put her hand to her mouth, and she sat there that way, not looking *at* Annie but *through* her, as if her niece wasn't really there and she was all by herself in the booth. "I don't believe it," she said yet again.

"I know I should have told you," Annie said anxiously. "But I didn't want to say anything in case I never heard from her. And then when I did hear from her I was so surprised that I wasn't sure how to tell you about it. Are you mad?"

The words had come out in a rush. When she was finished speaking Annie sat in the awful silence that followed and waited for an answer from Aunt Sarah. Finally, when Annie thought that for sure she would die if her aunt didn't say *something*, Aunt Sarah shook her head and seemed to come alive again.

"No," she said. "I'm not mad. It's just that it's been so long. Your mother and I used to talk sometimes about what she might be like. But we never thought—" She stopped talking, and Annie knew she was trying not to cry. "We never thought we would ever know," she said finally. Tears had formed in her eyes, and she blinked them back. "What's she like?" she asked Annie.

Annie sighed. Where should she begin? "Her name is Juliet Garrison," she said slowly. She looked at her aunt, gauging her reaction. "She's twenty-three. But you know that," she added, feeling foolish for forgetting.

"Juliet," Aunt Sarah repeated. "It's pretty."

"She lives in New Orleans," Annie continued. "She went to school there, and now she works as a costume designer for a theater company. I guess she inherited the whole artistic thing from Mom," she added.

Aunt Sarah smiled, which made Annie feel a lot better. "She was adopted by a family from Wisconsin," Annie said. "They had a farm. She grew up with five brothers and sisters. Three of them were adopted and three weren't. She's kind of in the middle, age-wise."

She wasn't sure what else to tell her aunt. She and Juliet had spoken about all kinds of things, but now that she was trying to tell Aunt Sarah about her, she found it difficult to put their conversations into words. Finally, her aunt made the decision for her and asked a question. "Is she happy?" she asked.

At first Annie thought this was a peculiar question. Then she looked at her aunt's face and saw the real question in her eyes. *She wants to know if my parents made the right decision*, she thought.

"Yes," she said. "She seems really happy. She loves her family, and she loves what she's doing now." She hesitated, thinking about something she and Juliet had talked about during their last phone call. "She says that she always felt a little different from them, though," she added. "That's why she contacted the adoption search people. She wondered what her birth family had been like, not because she was upset at them or anything but just because she wondered where she'd come from DNA-wise."

Aunt Sarah gave a short laugh. "If she only

knew," she said, smiling. She looked at Annie. "Part of me thinks I should be really angry with you," she said. "But I know that if I were you I would have done the same thing."

Annie grinned. "I know," she said. "And you wouldn't have told you, either."

"No," her aunt said, "I wouldn't. Now let me ask you a question: How do *you* feel about all of this?"

Annie thought about her answer for a minute. "Happy," she said. "At first I was shocked, and maybe a little angry at Mom and Dad. I don't know why, because I understand why they did what they did. But part of me felt like they'd taken this really big thing away from me. Now I feel like I've gotten it back, even though I haven't met her or anything."

There was a dramatic pause before Aunt Sarah asked, "Do you want to meet her?"

Annie nodded. "Yeah," she said. "I really do. And she wants to meet me—us—all of us."

"You haven't said anything to Meg, I take it," replied her aunt.

"Not a word," Annie answered. "I don't really know how to explain it to her."

Her aunt breathed out deeply. "*That* will be an interesting conversation," she said. "Maybe we should do it together. Have you and Juliet talked about when you might get together?"

"Well, that's something else I want to talk to you about," Annie said. "She suggested that maybe we come visit her for Mardi Gras."

"Mardi Gras?" Aunt Sarah said. "Isn't that, like, next week?"

"It's in March," Annie told her. "Juliet says it's really fun. We could stay with her and she'd show us around New Orleans and everything. What do you think? I have a week off for spring break anyway, so I wouldn't be missing school or anything."

Aunt Sarah was smiling.

"What's so funny?" Annie asked her, confused.

Her aunt shook her head. "Nothing," she answered. "It's just that I've never seen you want something so much before."

Annie blushed. The truth was, finding out she had a big sister had really affected her in ways she could never have imagined. She wanted to meet Juliet more than anything, and she realized that she'd been afraid that her aunt would say no for some reason.

"I think you should go," Aunt Sarah said. "I want to talk to Juliet first, of course," she added as Annie started to thank her.

Annie nodded emphatically. "Sure," she said.

"And I don't know if I'll be able to go myself," Aunt Sarah continued. "There's still a lot to do for the wedding. And I'm not sure if Meg should go yet," she added. "It might be best for you and Juliet to get to know each other first."

"Whatever you think is best," Annie said agreeably. She didn't want to say anything that might make her aunt change her mind.

Aunt Sarah took another sip of her milk shake. "Chloe would be so happy right now," she said.

Annie thought about that. What *would* her mother think if she knew her two older daughters were about to meet for the first time? Annie was pretty sure she would be okay with it. No, she *knew* she would be okay with it. But it made her sad to think that her mother would never get to know how her first child had turned out.

Oh, she knows, said a voice in her mind. *She and your father both know.*

Was that true? Annie wondered. She thought about the time she'd been able to speak to her parents' ghosts. Yes, they had been watching her grow up, they said. Had they also been able to watch Juliet grow up? Annie didn't know, but she hoped so. She wanted more than anything to believe that her parents knew that the little girl they'd given away was happy.

"Does Juliet's family know that she's found you?" Aunt Sarah asked, bringing Annie back to the moment.

"Yes," said Annie. "She told them that she was going to try to find her birth family. They were okay with that. I think it was hard for her to hear that Mom and Dad are dead."

Wait until she finds out you started the fire that killed them, said a familiar, taunting voice in her head. Annie had grown up with that voice, and had pretty much learned to ignore it, particularly since beginning her study of Wicca and coming to terms with the deaths of her mother and father. But from time to time it returned, teasing her, and at those times she felt like a six-year-old girl again, watching her house burn and knowing her parents were inside. She had, of course, told Juliet about the fire, but she hadn't revealed her role in it. She wasn't sure she was going to, either. At least not until she could talk to her sister face-to-face.

Her thoughts were interrupted by yet another squeal from a child sitting near their table. Her aunt looked at the child and then at Annie. "Ready to get out of here?" she asked.

"Big time," Annie replied, glad to leave. The fast food was sitting uneasily in her stomach, and she was happy to be away from the harsh colors and the noise.

They threw their trash away and left the restaurant. As the doors shut behind them Aunt Sarah put her arm around Annie and said, "Next time you have something important to tell me, can we do it at a nicer restaurant?"

They walked down the street, looking in the shop windows. They were standing in front of an Old Navy, admiring the endless array of eight-dollar T-shirts displayed in the window, when Annie heard someone call out her name. She turned and saw Kate, Cooper, Jane, and Sasha walking toward them.

"Hey," she said. "What are you guys up to?"

"It's Friday night," Sasha answered. "We thought

we'd hit a movie and scope out guys. Well, most of us would scope out guys," she added, glancing at Jane and grinning wickedly. Then she looked at Annie's aunt and made a face suggesting that she'd said the wrong thing. "I mean we thought we'd hit a movie," she amended.

"Please," Aunt Sarah said. "I'm not *that* old. And for your information, I know a thing or two about scoping out guys."

Annie's friends laughed.

"Do you want to come with us?" Kate asked Annie and her aunt. She turned to Aunt Sarah. "We could always use some guy-scoping hints."

"You go," Aunt Sarah said to Annie. "With Meg out of the house, I can enjoy a few hours on my own."

"Are you sure?" Annie asked. She really wanted to join her friends, but she didn't want to just dump her aunt like a bad date.

"I'm sure," Aunt Sarah said reassuringly. "Have a good time."

"Okay, then," Annie said. "I'll be back in a couple of hours."

"Take your time," her aunt said. "It's not often I get the place to myself." She waved good-bye and left the girls standing on the sidewalk.

"So, you were going to stand us up for something better, huh?" Cooper teased Annie.

"Yeah," Kate added. "We called your house to see if you wanted to come and there was no answer. Now we know why."

"It's a long story," Annie said. "I'll fill you in later."

It took a good twenty minutes of arguing before they settled on something they could all watch, but eventually they got into the movie and settled down. When they emerged ninety minutes later, some of them saying how great the movie was and the rest saying how bad it was, they stood outside debating what to do next.

"How about getting something to eat?" Cooper suggested. "Those licorice twists just didn't do it for me."

"I'm in," Kate said, and was immediately seconded by Jane and Annie.

"Sasha?" Cooper asked.

"Oh, um, I can't," said Sasha. "I told my mom I'd be home before eleven." She checked her watch. "I should go."

"Do you want a ride home?" Cooper asked her.

Sasha shook her head. "No," she said. "Don't worry about it. I'll be fine. I'll see you guys tomorrow, right?" she added. "At the bookstore?"

The others nodded. They had agreed to meet on Saturday morning at Crones' Circle, which was holding a one-day workshop on drumming. They were all looking forward to it.

"Okay," Sasha said. "'Bye."

She turned and walked away quickly. The others watched her for a minute. Then Cooper said, "She seemed like she was in an awful hurry, didn't she?"

"Just a little," agreed Jane. "What was that about?"

"Maybe she has a hot date," said Kate.

The others shot her looks.

"Well, maybe she does," said Kate. "You never know."

"Please," Annie said. "If Sasha had a hot date the whole *world* would know about it. Whatever it is, I'm sure we'll find out soon enough. Now, let's go eat, my stomach is demanding an apology for all of the Mc-junk I ate earlier."

CHAPTER 4

The broken glass that littered the floor was not the worst of it. That could be swept away—was, in fact, being swept away by Archer when the girls arrived at Crones' Circle the next morning for the workshop. Already most of it was in a pile, ready to be thrown into the waiting trash can.

"What happened?" Annie asked as she, Cooper, and Kate stood in the open doorway, looking around.

The store was a mess. Books had been thrown onto the floor. Shelves had been ransacked. Candles of all colors were scattered on the floor, and the jars of incense had been overturned, their multicolored powders blending together in a fragrant stain. Sophia stood by the cash register, looking at smashed cases that had once held jewelry—pentacles and Goddess pendants and silver rings—and at the open cash drawer in which nothing but a few loose coins remained.

"Somebody broke in last night," she said.

The girls entered the store, stepping over the broken glass and the spilled incense. Simeon, the big gray cat who called Crones' Circle his home, came out from beneath a bookcase and began rubbing against Cooper's leg.

"At least they didn't hurt Simi," said Sophia.

"Do you have any idea who did this?" asked Kate.

Sophia shook her head. "No," she said unhappily. "We left here at around ten o'clock last night and everything was fine. When Archer came in this morning to set up for the workshop, this is what she found."

"What about the alarm?" Cooper asked. "Why didn't it go off?"

"We're having a new one installed," answered Sophia. "The old one wasn't working." She surveyed her store, taking in the mess. "At least no one was hurt," she said, obviously trying to make the best of a bad situation. "That's the important thing."

"Hey, what's going on?"

The girls turned to see Sasha coming in. She was carrying a cup of coffee from the shop around the corner, and she was wearing sunglasses. When she saw the condition of the store she removed her glasses and let out a low whistle. "It must have been *some* party," she said.

"We'll help you clean up," said Annie to Sophia.

The girls all pitched in, returning books to the

shelves, straightening up what could be straightened, and throwing out what couldn't be salvaged. Within a short time the store looked a lot better, but it was still a bruised and battered version of its old self.

"It looks like they only took what they thought they could sell," remarked Cooper as they worked. "There are no books missing, just stuff like jewelry and cash."

"Whoever did it must have known the alarm wasn't working," Archer said. "No one would try to break into a store with an alarm system. They'd have to be nuts."

"Who knew about the alarm?" asked Annie.

"Just the repair guy and everyone who works here," answered Archer.

"That's a pretty short list," Cooper said. "Why would any of those people want to steal from the store?"

"That's what makes this so weird," remarked Sophia. "No one who works here *would* steal from the store. We all own it together. If someone steals, she's really only stealing from herself."

"Maybe someone was watching the place and noticed that you weren't setting an alarm when you left at night," suggested Sasha as she restacked a table of books.

"Maybe," Sophia said. "It doesn't really matter, though. What's done is done. All we can do is go forward."

"You have insurance though, right?" asked Sasha. "I mean, this is all covered?"

Sophia shook her head. "Our policy doesn't cover theft," she said. "We save money by having a very basic policy. So this all comes out of our pockets."

Sasha frowned. "Oh," she said quietly, and went back to cleaning up.

"I just can't believe someone would do something like this," Kate said. "It makes me so angry. I wish we could do a spell or something to teach the person a lesson."

Archer put an arm around Kate as she walked past carrying the broom. "Didn't you learn *your* lesson about putting spells on people the hard way?" she joked.

Kate blushed. "You know what I mean," she said. "I just hate to see whoever did this get away with it."

"You never really get away with anything," said Sophia. "Remember what the Law of Three says: whatever energy you put out comes back to you three times as strong. I imagine that whoever broke into the store is really hurting." She looked around the store. "But that doesn't mean I wouldn't like to tell that person a thing or two."

"You missed some great pizza last night after you left," said Kate, turning to Sasha. "We talked Cooper into trying the White Russian at Pie in the Sky. *Tons* of cheese."

"Yeah, and thanks to all of that cheese I had the worst dreams last night," remarked Cooper testily.

"Oh, it couldn't possibly be all of the calamari you had first, could it?" Annie teased. "You were eating so much squid you looked like a shark in a feeding frenzy."

Cooper shot Annie an evil look. "I wouldn't talk if I were you, Miss Mozzarella Fingers," she said. She held up her hand and wiggled her fingers at Annie menacingly.

"Okay, everything looks a million times better," said Sophia, sounding a little less stressed out than she had half an hour before. "People should be arriving for the workshop any minute. Why don't you all help Archer set up the back room?"

"You mean you're still going to hold the workshop?" Kate asked.

Sophia nodded. "We can't let a little thing like this shut us down," she said. "We'll get something to cover the broken glass in the door and keep out the cold, but otherwise we are open for business." She stressed the final three words as though making an official declaration.

The girls joined Archer in the rear of the store and helped her set cushions all around the room. A few minutes later the workshop leader—a tall, thin African American woman—came in carrying her hand drum in a padded case slung across her back.

"Toni!" Archer exclaimed, giving the woman a big hug. "It's great to see you again."

"Same here," said the woman, whose hair was a mass of dreadlocks and whose arms rippled with muscle as she set her drum down. "How long has it been?"

"Since last year's Wise Woman festival," Archer said. "Remember, it rained all weekend and we finally decided we'd had enough of being in the lodge so we did the spiral dance in the middle of a thunderstorm?"

Toni laughed. "Right," she said. "And if I recall, *you* were the one who suggested that everyone cover themselves in mud and jump in the lake afterward."

"It was *very* primal," Archer said to the girls, who were listening raptly.

"What happened here?" asked Toni. "It looks like someone played hardball with your front door."

"We had a little intrusion last night," explained Archer.

Toni shook her head. "It's a sad day when someone will rob a little bookstore like this when there's a great big chain bookstore filled with cash sitting right across the street," she said. Then she looked at the others. "I'm just kidding, of course," she added seriously.

Everybody laughed at her joke. Toni nodded appreciatively. "Keep it up," she said. "I like a crowd that thinks I'm funny."

"What are we going to do today?" Annie asked her.

"Have you ever drummed before?" Toni inquired.

Annie shook her head. "I've always wanted to, though," she said.

"Here's your chance," said Toni, handing her the drum she'd just removed from its case. "Play me something."

Annie turned red. "I can't," she said. "I don't know how. Cooper is the musician."

"Cooper?" Toni said, cocking her head. "Which one of you is Cooper?"

"That would be me," Cooper said, raising her hand. "But I play guitar, not drums."

Toni squinted her eyes at them. "I think you're all just a little shy," she said. "Okay, then, I'll start."

She picked up the drum and began slapping her palms against it, making all kinds of different sounds. It really sounded as if the drum was talking to them, and they all stood, transfixed, as she played for a couple of minutes.

"That's what you'll be able to do when I'm through with you all," she said, grinning.

The others looked at her doubtfully, but there was no time to argue as the other workshop participants began to file in and take their places. The girls took theirs as well and waited expectantly until everyone was there and Toni began the class.

After a few welcoming remarks she launched into her presentation.

"The Goddess loves to dance," she told her audience as she began to play a gentle rhythm. "And she especially likes to dance to a good beat." She changed her hand movements, resulting in strong tapping that sounded like a proud woman stepping confidently. "When you play the drums, try to imagine your favorite goddess dancing to it. Imagine her swinging her skirts and throwing her head back."

Toni played for a while as the class participants nodded their heads and clapped their hands along with her. Then she stopped and looked at all of them. "And now it's time for you to play," she said. She nodded to a number of drums that Archer had set up on one side of the room. "Each of you pick a drum," she said. "There are enough to go around."

They all stood up and walked to the drums, looking them over and choosing the one that appealed to them most. Then they returned to their places and sat with the drums in their laps.

"The first thing you need to learn is that your drum is not a baby," Toni said. "Don't be afraid of hurting it. You're all holding on to those things like they're newborn infants."

People laughed as Toni showed them the correct way to hold their drums. Then she began by teaching them basic hand movements, which they copied until she was satisfied that they were all doing them more or less correctly. Fairly quickly they were all playing easy rhythms.

"See," said Toni. "I told you all that you could do it."

The whole time they were playing, Kate noticed that Sasha kept looking at her watch. "Do you need to be somewhere?" she asked her friend.

Sasha shook her head. "Just checking the time," she said. "I was hoping lunch was coming up."

As if that were a cue, Toni told them they could stop playing. "We'll break for lunch now," she said, putting her drum down. "Eat up, because when we come back we're going to *jam*."

The girls set their drums carefully to the side and gathered in the middle of the room to decide where to go for lunch.

"No pizza," Cooper said automatically.

"How about sandwiches at the deli down the street?" suggested Kate.

That idea met with everyone's approval, and the girls left the store and headed for the deli. Once there, they stood in line and debated what to have. Sasha approached the counter first.

"Give me a roast beef and cheese on sourdough," she said. "With the works. And also give me a turkey breast on whole wheat with honey mustard, Swiss, and tomato. Hold the lettuce. Oh, and two bottled waters."

"Wow," Cooper said. "I guess you really worked up an appetite doing all that drumming."

"Yeah," Sasha answered. "I guess I did."

When her sandwiches came, Sasha took the bag and turned to the others. "I'll meet you back at the store in a little while," she said. "I have some errands I have to run for Thea. You know, pick-up-stuff-at-the-drugstore kinds of things."

"What about your lunch?" asked Annie, who was paying for her ham and cheese on rye. "You have to eat."

"Oh, I will," Sasha assured her. "I can eat and walk at the same time. See ya."

She left the store—and her friends—and headed down the street. Cooper looked at the others, raising one eyebrow. "Am I the only one who thinks that girl is up to something?" she asked.

"No," Annie said. "You're not."

"Am I the only one who thinks we should follow her and see where she's going?" Cooper tried.

Kate and Annie looked at one another. They were holding their bags of lunch in their hands.

"No," Kate said. "You're not."

"Let's go," Cooper declared, heading for the door.

They walked in the direction Sasha had gone. They could see her about half a block ahead of them, moving fast and dodging around anyone who got in her way.

"Wherever she's going, she's definitely in a hurry," Annie said.

"Well, there are no drugstores up this way that I can remember," said Cooper as they headed away from the main shopping area. "In fact, there's not much up here at all."

They followed Sasha as she made her way to the park that sat at the edge of the shopping district. In the summer the park was filled with people walking, playing, and enjoying the weather. In the February chill it was deserted. But Sasha walked right into it as if there was something she needed to see, and right away.

Kate, Annie, and Cooper hung back, not wanting Sasha to spot them if she turned around. But she seemed completely focused on moving forward, never looking back to see if she was being followed or watched. She walked straight through the park to the area where, in nicer weather, a huge fountain splashed into the air, filling a large surrounding pool with water. Now, with the water turned off, the fountain was filled mainly with dead leaves and garbage.

Sasha stopped at the fountain and looked around. Her friends hid behind a large tree and peered around it at her, waiting to see what she was doing. Sasha paced uneasily, checking her watch frequently and scanning the surrounding area.

"What is she doing?" Annie whispered.

"Whatever it is, I have a feeling it's *not* good," Cooper answered.

"Do you think she's buying drugs?" suggested Kate. "I mean, this area is kind of known for that."

No one said anything. The truth was, they didn't know a lot about Sasha's past. She was a runaway, and they knew she'd had a pretty tough life on the streets. While none of them thought their friend would do anything like take drugs, the fact was they weren't totally sure she wouldn't. But none of them wanted to say so, and so they stood silently and watched.

"There," Annie said a minute later. "Look."

Cooper and Kate looked where Annie was pointing and saw someone walking toward Sasha. It was a girl. She seemed nervous, looking around a lot and constantly playing with the sunglasses she wore even though it was a cloudy day.

"She looks kind of dirty," said Annie, noting the girl's not-very-clean jeans and the dingy T-shirt she wore beneath an old hooded sweatshirt.

The girl walked up to Sasha and they talked for a moment. Then Sasha handed her the bag from the deli. The girl reached inside, pulled out one of the sandwiches, and began eating. She crammed the food into her mouth rapidly, letting pieces of it spill out onto the ground.

"You'd think she'd never eaten before," said Kate, watching her.

Sasha was talking to the girl, who seemed

more interested in what else the bag held than in talking back. They could see Sasha was getting frustrated. She was waving her hands in the air and gesturing pointedly. But the girl just unwrapped the second sandwich and started working on that. Finally, Sasha poked her in the shoulder.

The girl stepped back and glared at Sasha. She said something the girls couldn't hear. Then she stuck her hand in the pocket of the grungy jeans and pulled something out. She handed it to Sasha, who looked at it and put it into her own pocket.

"That didn't look like drugs," remarked Annie.

"And I don't think most dealers would take sandwiches in payment anyway," Cooper added.

Sasha was talking again, but this time the girl turned and walked away from her. Sasha called out to her. "Hey," she shouted, loud enough for her friends to hear. "I help you out and this is what I get? Fine. Next time you're on your own."

The girl ignored her and kept going. Sasha stormed off as well, walking toward the girls' hiding place.

"Let's get out of here," Cooper said. "If she sees us we're in big trouble."

They turned and ran back the way they'd come. They moved quickly, needing to stay ahead of Sasha. By the time they made it back to the shopping area they were winded and sweating.

"We don't have time to eat these," Cooper said, holding up her lunch bag. "We'll have to toss them or she'll know we were up to something."

"But I'm *hungry*," Kate complained.

Cooper snatched Kate's bag and threw it, along with her own, into the nearest trash can. "I'll buy you dinner after class," she said. "Now, let's go."

CHAPTER 5

Cooper picked up the empty bottle and carried it into the kitchen, where she dropped it unceremoniously into the trash can, listening to it clatter against the other bottles already in there. She was tempted to take the bottles out and count them. When had she last emptied the trash? Thursday? There had been four bottles in there then. How many were there now? She stared at the trash can for a moment and then turned off the kitchen lights and walked out.

It was Sunday morning. Her mother was in bed, sleeping or passed out, Cooper wasn't sure which. Cooper had come home on Saturday night after a date with T.J. to find the living room a mess and her mother sitting in an armchair, staring angrily at the picture of herself, Cooper, and Mr. Rivers that sat on the mantelpiece. When Cooper had said hello, her mother had turned her haunted eyes to her daughter and said something Cooper couldn't understand, but the meaning had been all too clear:

her mother wasn't happy to see her.

Fighting her natural inclination to simply retreat to her room, Cooper had insisted on helping her mother stand up and walk upstairs to her bedroom. She'd gotten her mother into bed before shutting her bedroom door and going back downstairs to have a look around. The house had smelled to her like alcohol, anger, and fear. She'd wanted to open all of the windows and air it out, but finally she'd just gone to bed. She was exhausted after her long day, and she needed some rest.

She'd slept badly, plagued by disturbing dreams in which she kept trying to locate a lost kitten that she could hear crying but that she could never find. She'd woken up at dawn feeling more tired and out of sorts than when she'd gone to bed, and finally she'd just gotten up. Now she was doing what she'd thought of doing the night before, cleaning the house.

Despite the fact that it was freezing outside, Cooper had opened the windows in the living room, putting on an old, comfortable sweater to keep herself from getting chilled. She was actually enjoying the breeze that was sweeping through the room, ridding it of the unpleasant scent that had permeated it lately. It felt to Cooper like cleaning a big cage, a cage that had held a wounded and unhappy animal. Unfortunately, that animal was her mother, and she was going to have to do something about her.

The question was: What? How could she possibly help someone who, in the grand scheme of things, was supposed to help *her* when she was in trouble? She didn't know how to *talk* to her mother most of the time, let alone try to help her with something this serious. The truth was, Cooper was scared. Her mother had always been one of those people who had everything under control. Even though she and Cooper rarely agreed on anything, Cooper had always counted on her mother to be dependable, even in her stubbornness and intractability. But since she'd begun drinking, the old Janet Rivers had been replaced by an ugly version of herself, a version Cooper wanted to run away from, not help.

She thought about calling her father again. He had tried to help once before. But he was part of the problem. Cooper's mother had begun drinking because of the stress she felt about their divorce. Cooper knew that if her father tried to intervene again it would just make everything worse. She needed someone else. But who? Did she even know anyone who was stable and dependable anymore?

A list of names rolled silently through her head: Sophia, Archer, Thea, Thatcher. They would all help her in a minute if she asked. But they were all part of her Wiccan life. Cooper knew that her involvement in witchcraft was not something her mother found at all reassuring. Asking her Wiccan friends to get involved would probably make everything worse. *No, it would* definitely *make everything worse,* she thought. She needed to look elsewhere.

Another list of names came to her: Annie's Aunt Sarah and Kate's mother and father. They were all people Cooper admired. And again, she knew that any of them would probably be glad to help her out. But none of them seemed quite right. She needed someone who was kind but tough, who would listen but not be pushed around.

Suddenly it came to her. Mrs. McAllister, T.J.'s mom. Mary McAllister was one of the most good-hearted people Cooper had ever met. Cooper also knew that Mrs. McAllister had had her own experiences with people who drank too much, having come from a family where alcohol was as common as water at the dinner table. T.J. had told Cooper some of the stories, and they'd made Cooper very sad. They'd also made Cooper even more in awe of the way Mrs. McAllister seemed to welcome the world in with open arms, never judging and always ready to give a hug or a kind word. In some ways Cooper thought of Mrs. McAllister as another mother. She knew she could talk to her.

She glanced at the clock. It was only seven, but she knew that T.J.'s mother would be up. She never slept past six, and by the time the rest of her sleepy family stumbled downstairs she had usually been busy for several hours.

Cooper pulled a jacket on over her sweater, left the windows open so that the house could breathe, and went to her car. She drove to the McAllisters' house and parked. Sure enough, the lights in the kitchen were on, shining through the gray February morning. Cooper felt better just looking at them.

She got out and went to the front door. She didn't want to knock, in case the McAllisters' old Irish setter, Mac, decided it was one of his infrequent times to act like the guard dog he supposedly was and bark. But she also didn't want to just walk in and potentially startle Mrs. McAllister.

She walked around to the kitchen window and peered in. Just as she'd suspected, T.J.'s mom was in the kitchen. She was stirring something in a big mixing bowl, and she was talking to herself. *She probably has the radio on*, thought Cooper. Mrs. McAllister loved to listen to the radio, particularly the stations that played music by people like Frank Sinatra and Judy Garland. She had a pleasant voice—T.J. had inherited his singing talents from her—and Cooper liked listening to her. Now, though, she wished Mrs. McAllister would stop singing and look her way.

She tapped on the window gently. Mrs. McAllister looked around, but not out the window. Cooper knocked a little harder. This time T.J.'s mom did look out. Cooper saw her squinch up her eyes, trying to make out who was standing outside her kitchen window. Mrs. McAllister came closer. *She's not afraid of anything*, Cooper thought. Anyone else, hearing someone tapping on their window in the early hours of a Sunday morning, would probably have reached for a shotgun or phoned the police. Mrs. McAllister, though, just looked until she realized who was out there.

The kitchen door opened a moment later. "Get your butt in here," said Mrs. McAllister. "It's freezing."

Cooper went inside. Immediately she was engulfed in the warmth of the kitchen and the smell of blueberry muffins. Mrs. McAllister motioned for her to take off her coat. "Sit down," she said.

"Sorry about the Peeping Tom routine," said Cooper. "I didn't want Mac to sound the alarm."

"You needn't have worried," said Mrs. McAllister. "He's asleep on T.J.'s bed. They're both snoring like a couple of freight trains."

Cooper laughed. Already she felt better. The difference between her house and the McAllisters' was amazing. Here she felt at home, as if she could be herself without worrying that someone was going to come along to make her feel bad. At home she was always on edge, waiting for something unpleasant to happen.

Mrs. McAllister handed her a plate with a blueberry muffin on it. Cooper split open the muffin and watched steam emerge, carrying with it the sweet scent of the berries.

"Coffee?" Mrs. McAllister asked. She was the only person Cooper had ever met who offered teenagers coffee. It always made Cooper feel very grown up for some reason, and even though she didn't particularly like coffee, she always accepted.

"Sure," she said. "Thanks."

Mrs. McAllister fetched two cups and filled them with coffee from the pot that was continuously brewing on the coffeemaker. Everyone in the McAllister house drank coffee, so the pot was constantly being refilled. Cooper had the vague suspicion that as babies the McAllister boys had all had coffee in their bottles, which would, she thought, explain why they were all just a little bit on the eccentric side. "It's all that caffeine," she sometimes said to T.J. when he was being particularly difficult. "It did something to your brain."

Mrs. McAllister set the cups on the table and pulled out a chair. She sat down, took a sip of coffee, and said, "I take it you're not here to see my son."

"No," said Cooper. "This is kind of about me."

Mrs. McAllister nodded but didn't say anything. Cooper knew that she *wouldn't* say anything. She would wait for Cooper to tell her what was on her mind. It was how she operated—maintaining a patient yet demanding silence that forced the other person to speak. It was a technique she'd perfected on her husband and her four sons. T.J.'d told Cooper that when they were little he and his brothers could never keep secrets from their mother. Whenever she suspected that information was being withheld, she would simply sit them down at the table and wait them out. Inevitably, and usually after a lot of squirming and fidgeting on his part, whichever boy was the subject of her unbearable silence would blurt out the truth, however embarrassing it was. "There," she would always say, not rubbing her victory in but clearly enjoying her success, "was that so hard?"

Cooper decided not to prolong the wait. "It's my mother," she said. "She's drinking a lot, and I'm worried about her. I want to do something, but I don't know what I can do. When I try to talk to her she just turns her back on me. My father can't do anything because he's part of the problem. I feel like I'm trapped in my own house. I'm afraid to say the wrong thing or do the wrong thing, and I have this constant ache in my stomach from worrying about it."

It was the longest speech Cooper had ever made to Mrs. McAllister. The more she talked, the more came out. It felt good to say the things she was saying, but it also made her very sad. It was as if getting the words out had unlocked a door to the place inside of her where she hid her feelings from everyone. There were a lot of them stored in there, like boxes piled one on top of another, and now their contents spilled out. She found herself holding back tears. And then she found that she couldn't hold those back, either. She began to cry, and before she could stop herself she was sobbing quietly in Mrs. McAllister's warm kitchen while from the radio came the sound of the Andrews Sisters singing "Ac-Cent-Tchu-Ate the Positive."

T.J.'s mother stood up and came to stand behind Cooper. She put her big, soft arms around Cooper's neck and kissed her gently on the top of the head. "There," she said, "was that so hard?"

Cooper laughed in spite of herself. She put her hand on one of Mrs. McAllister's and sat, just holding it while her tears subsided. She breathed deeply a few times, calming herself. "No," she said when she could speak, although her voice trembled. "It wasn't so hard."

Mrs. McAllister sat down again. She picked up her coffee cup, looked inside, and then got up and poured herself some more. She drank some, smiled, and then said, "It has nothing to do with you. You know that, right?"

Cooper nodded. "I know," she said. "That's not the problem."

"Good," said T.J.'s mother. "For a long time I thought my father's drinking *was* my fault." She paused. "Probably because he told me it was," she added, laughing.

Cooper laughed, too. She was amazed at how easily Mrs. McAllister could talk about what Cooper was sure must have been a very painful childhood. She knew from what T.J. had told her that Mrs. McAllister's father had often beaten her and her siblings when he was in a drunken rage. Twice he had sent her to the hospital needing stitches, and her mother had taken her, telling the nurses that Mary had fallen down the stairs or had an accident with her bike and promising her some kind of present if she didn't tell anyone the truth.

"People drink because they don't like who they are," she said. "My father didn't like the man he was. He thought the one he was when he was drunk was better. Stronger, maybe, or at least not so afraid. I don't think he meant to hurt any of us. I don't think he wanted to, deep down. He could be the kindest man you ever met," she said, smiling faintly. "But not when he had been drinking."

"I'm not afraid of my mother or anything," Cooper told her. "I mean, I don't think she'll do anything like what your father did."

"There are all kinds of hurt, honey," Mrs. McAllister said quietly. "All kinds of hurt."

"I just don't want her to do anything to herself," Cooper continued. "How do I get her to stop?"

"*You* don't get her to stop," Mrs. McAllister said. "She has to get herself to stop."

"Okay," Cooper said. "So how do I get her to stop herself, then?"

T.J.'s mother smiled. "You are a determined one," she said. She took a piece of Cooper's forgotten muffin and put it in her own mouth. She chewed quietly for a minute, then resumed speaking. "People stop drinking when they're ready to stop," she said. "Not before. My father didn't stop drinking till the day he died, and I wouldn't be surprised to find out he snuck a bottle into the casket with him. He never was ready to stop. Other people are luckier. They figure out that it's not getting them anywhere and they decide to find another way to face whatever it is that's eating at them. That's what I did."

"You?" Cooper said, surprised. T.J. had never mentioned to her that his mother had ever had a problem with drinking.

"Surprised?" asked Mrs. McAllister.

Cooper nodded. "Yeah," she said. "I mean, after your father and all—" She stopped, realizing that what she was about to say was probably out of line.

"Seeing someone else fall down doesn't always stop you from trying to do the same stupid thing they were doing," Mrs. McAllister said. "See, I thought my father just couldn't handle drinking. I thought I could. But I was his daughter in more ways than one."

Cooper tried to imagine Mrs. McAllister drunk. She couldn't even picture the smiling, loving woman sitting beside her ever having a problem with alcohol. She seemed so together, so solid. *So does Mom sometimes*, she thought suddenly.

"After Dylan was born, I went into a depression," Mrs. McAllister told her. "I thought I was probably going to be the worst mother that ever lived. Really, I think, I was afraid that I was going to become *my* mother. I'd never really faced how I felt about her all those years. Anyway, having a few drinks made things easier. And pretty soon a few drinks became a lot of drinks." She nodded thoughtfully. "It doesn't take a lot," she told Cooper. "Everybody thinks it takes years and years, but it doesn't."

Cooper thought about her own mother. Cooper had seen her drink before, but she'd never seen her drunk or even close to it. Now, though, Mrs. Rivers seemed constantly to have a drink in her hand and another one waiting for when she was through with the first. Had she become an alcoholic overnight? That was really hard to think about.

"Why did you finally stop?" Cooper asked T.J.'s mother. She knew it was probably a rude question, but she really wanted to know what had made Mrs. McAllister realize that she was hurting herself.

"One afternoon I was giving Dylan a bath," answered T.J.'s mother. "The water was too hot, but I didn't realize it because I was a little numb at the time. He'd been crying a lot that day, and I'd had a few drinks to—as I told myself—take the edge off. When I put him in the water it burned him, not badly but enough to turn him red and make him cry. I thought I'd really hurt him, so I took him to the emergency room. When the doctor asked me what had happened, I told him that the baby-sitter was responsible, that she had carelessly allowed my baby to be put into water that was too hot." She looked at Cooper. "When I heard myself say that, I heard my mother making up all of those excuses for what my father had done to us. I looked at Dylan, who was fine, and I wondered what the next excuse I'd have to make up might be. That was enough to stop me cold."

"And you just quit drinking?" Cooper asked.

Mrs. McAllister got up to get more coffee for

both of them. "Well, it wasn't quite that easy," she said. "I had some help. I went to AA meetings."

"Alcoholics Anonymous?" Cooper said.

"You sound a little shocked," remarked Mrs. McAllister.

Cooper shrugged. "It's just that I always thought AA was for, you know—"

"Winos and hard-core drunks?" asked T.J.'s mother, raising an eyebrow.

"Well, yeah," admitted Cooper. She felt horrible, as if she'd somehow offended Mrs. McAllister.

Mrs. McAllister smiled. "Don't worry," she said. "That's what most people think. I met a lot of wonderful people there, people who are still friends of mine. And going to those meetings helped me see that alcohol wasn't the problem, it was the symptom of the problem. What I really feared was becoming like my parents and hurting my family the way they had hurt us."

"My mother would never go to an AA meeting," said Cooper. "Not in a million years."

"Maybe not," agreed Mrs. McAllister. "But maybe she'd have coffee with me."

"You'd do that?" asked Cooper.

"For the girl who puts up with my son? Anything," Mrs. McAllister answered.

The two of them were laughing when T.J. walked in, sleepily rubbing his eyes. When he saw Cooper sitting at the kitchen table with his mother he looked at her as if he thought he was dreaming.

He kept looking from his mother to his girlfriend and back again.

"I don't even want to know," he said. "Do I?"

"I was just giving Cooper my muffin recipe," Mrs. McAllister said seriously, sending both her and Cooper into a new round of laughter.

"I was right," said T.J., taking a muffin from the plate on the counter and turning and walking out of the kitchen. "I don't want to know."

CHAPTER 6

"You're putting too much dirt in."

Kate shot Sherrie a glance. Kate was putting dirt into little planting pots, and Sherrie was watching her. She hadn't made a move to help, claiming that she didn't want to ruin the manicure she'd gotten the day before, but she'd taken every possible opportunity to inform Kate that she was doing it all wrong.

"It's not too much dirt," said Kate evenly. "It's *fine.*"

"There's no room for the seeds to grow," Sherrie said, as if she knew everything in the world there was to know about plants and was graciously sharing her knowledge with Kate. "They'll smother in all that dirt."

"Sherrie, when was the last time you planted anything?" asked Kate, setting the pot on the lab table and reaching for the package of seeds.

"I helped my mother with our garden last year, for your information," Sherrie said haughtily. "And we took first prize in her garden club competition."

"For your roses, Sherrie," Kate said moodily. "Which you didn't grow from seeds—your mother had shrubs planted, and she has a *gardener* who comes in every week."

Sherrie didn't respond. She just looked at her nails, as if somehow a tiny piece of dirt had managed to get onto one of them and completely ruined her entire life.

Kate looked at the seed packet. They were going to grow marigolds, and Kate wanted to see how deep the seeds needed to be buried in the dirt.

"These need to go a quarter inch into the soil," she informed Sherrie, who seemed about as interested in this piece of information as she might be about hearing that the stock market was up or down.

"So?" Sherrie said. "I am *not* putting my fingers in dirt. Didn't I already explain that?" She let out an exasperated sigh, as if Kate were some kind of very slow child to whom she had explained a simple concept three hundred times without success.

"You don't need to use your fingers," said Kate. She picked up a pencil and handed it to Sherrie. "Start poking," she ordered.

Holding the pencil as if it were a live snake, Sherrie halfheartedly began making indentations in the twenty-four little pots of soil that Kate had filled. Kate, meanwhile, took as long as possible to rip the top off the package of marigold seeds. She was thinking about the black candle she'd done the ritual around. It was sitting on her altar at home. Every night, while she did homework or read, she burned it and imagined her dislike of Sherrie burning away into the ether. The candle was about a third of the way gone now.

But the spell wasn't working. The candle was getting shorter and shorter, but it didn't seem to be taking any of Kate's negative feelings with it. Every night she tried dutifully to let go of the anger she felt, and for a while it seemed that she did have a more positive outlook on having to work with Sherrie on the experiment.

Then, however, she would see Sherrie live and in person and be filled once again with the almost overwhelming desire to kick her in the shins. All Sherrie had to do was look at her sideways and all of Kate's Wiccan-white-light-positive-energy feelings evaporated like drops of water on a hot stove. The old familiar animosity returned, shoving the good stuff out of the way and settling down for a long stay.

Kate wasn't sure what to do about this. On the one hand, she didn't care if she and Sherrie ever got along again. But she needed to get a good grade on the project, which meant that she had to at least refrain from totally alienating Sherrie until they were done, which wouldn't be for another month. Besides, she really did want to see if she could learn how to get rid of any negative feelings she might have about someone. She knew that the exercise was a good one for her to attempt. It was another challenge on her path.

But why couldn't I have had something easier? she asked herself. *Like turning straw into gold.*

Sherrie had finished making holes in the dirt. Not surprisingly, she had done a terrible job of it. Glancing at the pots, Kate could see that in some of them Sherrie had barely made an indentation in the dirt, while in others she appeared to have been trying to dig a hole to China, pushing the pencil practically to the bottom of the pot.

Deep breaths, Kate told herself. *White light in, black light out.*

She began to place the marigold seeds in the holes, repairing the damage Sherrie had done to the dirt as she did so. She put a few seeds in each pot.

"That's too many seeds," said Sherrie critically. "How are they all supposed to grow in those little pots?"

"They won't all grow," Kate explained as patiently as she could. "Only some of them will. And if more than one does, we just pluck out the weakest one and throw it away." She looked meaningfully at Sherrie as she said the last part of her statement. *I'd love to just pluck her and throw her away,* she thought.

"Why couldn't we use prettier plants?" Sherrie asked." Marigolds are so common."

"They're easy to grow," said Kate. "And they

72

grow quickly. This way we can get our results faster and we won't have to drag this out *any longer than we have to*." She emphasized her last words so that Sherrie would know what she was really saying. The sooner they were finished, the sooner they could stop being nice to one another.

"Well, in that case," said Sherrie, as if she had decided out of the goodness of her heart to allow Kate to use marigolds after all.

Kate covered the seeds with dirt and tapped it down to fill in any little air pockets that might have formed. Then she took a beaker, filled it with water, and watered half the plants. Six of these she set onto a tray. The other six went onto another tray. The unwatered plants were also divided into two groups of six and placed on their own trays.

"What's that about?" asked Sherrie.

"Didn't you even read the instructions?" Kate asked her, irritated.

"Of course I read them," Sherrie snapped. "Plant seeds."

Kate huffed angrily. "The point of this experiment is to try growing plants under different conditions," she said. "Six of them will get lots of water and lots of light. Six will get lots of water and very little light. Six will get very little water and lots of light. And the last six will get very little water and very little light. Every day we'll record their progress and see which conditions produce the best plants."

"Who cares?" asked Sherrie. "You can just buy marigolds at the nursery. They're like a hundred for a dollar or something."

Kate closed her eyes and gritted her teeth. She counted backward from ten. She imagined a whole ocean of white light filling her up and pushing her black, negative feelings out. The feelings exploded like a huge nuclear mushroom cloud. She imagined it wiping Sherrie off the face of the earth. She knew this was the wrong approach to take, but it made her feel better.

"It doesn't matter how stupid the experiment is or isn't," she said slowly, trying not to let her voice rise. "We just have to do it."

"Whatever," said Sherrie. "Are we done?"

"Yes," Kate said. "We're done for now. But we have to make a schedule for monitoring how the plants are doing and for watering them and turning on the grow light."

Sherrie sighed and rolled her eyes. "Fine," she said. "But I'm really, really busy with stuff right now, so don't expect me to do all the work."

"I wouldn't think of it," replied Kate. "I'll make up a schedule and give it to you tomorrow. And I promise not to make it too taxing. I know you have a busy social life to worry about."

"Gee," Sherrie said. "I'm really sorry you decided to stop being popular and all, but that's no reason to get nasty about it. I'm *trying* to make the best of this. I would think you would, too."

The best of this would be if I crammed all twenty-four pots of dirt down your throat, thought Kate, but she didn't say anything. Instead she picked up two of the trays and headed for the grow lights. When she turned around, Sherrie was gone.

"I wish it was always that easy to get rid of her," said Kate out loud.

"Trouble in paradise?"

Kate turned around to see Sasha standing in the doorway to the science lab. "I was just on my way to Spanish," she explained. "I saw Sherrie storm out of here and thought I'd see if you were okay."

"Yeah," Kate said as she put away the remaining two trays of plants and grabbed her books. "I'm okay."

She walked with Sasha as they headed for their next classes. Kate hadn't seen Sasha since Saturday afternoon. She hadn't been in any of their shared classes that morning, and Kate had wondered where she was. Now she asked.

"Oh," Sasha replied in answer to the question. "I had a dentist appointment this morning." She chomped her teeth together noisily. "All clean," she said.

They reached Sasha's Spanish class and Kate said good-bye. As she continued on to the gym she thought about what had happened over the weekend. She, Annie, and Cooper had gone over and over it, and the three of them had a suspicion that somehow Sasha had been involved in the break-in at Crones'

Circle. They didn't know why, but the evidence sure pointed in her direction: the way she'd left them all so suddenly on Friday night, her inability to give them a straight answer about where she was, and especially the meeting with the weird girl in the park on Saturday. It all added up to trouble for Sasha.

The girls hadn't said anything to her, or to Sophia and the others at the bookstore. They were trying to figure out the best way to handle things. Sasha had been through a lot in her life. No one knew the full story behind why she'd run away or what had happened to her while she lived on the streets. She'd really turned her life around since coming to Beecher Falls, and particularly since becoming involved with the Wiccan community and being adopted by Thea. None of her friends wanted to believe that she was falling into her old ways again. But maybe she was. After all, it was hard to ignore what they'd seen with their own eyes.

"Hey."

Kate looked around. Cooper and Annie were waving to her from the side hallway.

"Come here," Cooper said.

Kate went over to the two of them. "What are you guys doing here?" she asked. "You're supposed to be in class."

"We decided to do some investigating," said Annie.

"Investigating?" Kate said. "What? Is this some

article you're working on for the school paper?"

"No," Annie said. "It's a little closer to home. Come on."

She and Cooper turned and walked away. Kate glanced back toward the gym, where she was supposed to be suiting up to play basketball with Jessica and Tara, and then followed her friends. They walked down the hall and turned, heading for the lockers.

"This had better be good," said Kate as they walked. "Tara and Jess aren't going to be thrilled that I skipped on them."

"Oh, it's good," Cooper told her.

"Or bad, depending how you look at it," Annie said.

They turned into the bays and Cooper began fumbling with the combination lock on one of the lockers.

"Hey," Kate said. "That's Sasha's locker."

"We know," Annie said, watching Cooper.

"How do you know the combination?" Kate asked, looking over Cooper's shoulder.

"She gave it to me once when she was out sick and needed me to bring her some books," Cooper explained, giving the lock a final turn and pulling up on the handle. The locker slid open easily. "I just happened to remember it," she added, giving Kate a wink.

"But why are we looking in here at all?" Kate

asked. "That's *so* an invasion of privacy."

"We had probable cause," Annie said. "And we turned out to be right."

Cooper reached into Sasha's locker and pulled out a small zippered bag. She handed it to Kate. "Go on," she said. "Take a look."

Kate looked at the bag in her hand. It was heavy, and when she shook it there was a soft jingling sound from inside. "What is it?" she asked her friends.

"*Look*," Cooper said again.

Kate unzipped the bag and peered into it. Then she reached in and pulled out a handful of rings and pendants. "These are from the bookstore!" she said, looking at the pentacles and goddesses in her hand.

"Bingo," Annie said. "That's the missing jewelry."

"Well, some of it," said Cooper. "And there's something else." She reached into the bag and pulled out a wad of cash. "There's this."

Kate groaned and leaned against the lockers. She handed Cooper the bag. Holding it made her feel even worse. "What are we going to do?" she asked.

"We're going to have to tell somebody," Cooper answered.

"Shouldn't we talk to her first?" said Kate. "Maybe she's in trouble."

"I'll say she's in trouble," Annie remarked. "Big trouble."

None of them said anything for a minute as they

all stared at the bag in Cooper's hand. It was as if they were trying to make it disappear so that they wouldn't have to deal with it. Finally, Cooper broke the silence. "I'm sure there's an explanation," she said. "Even if it isn't one we want to hear."

"Yes," said a voice behind them. "There is an explanation. Whether or not you want to hear it is up to you."

They turned and saw Sasha watching them. Her eyes blazed with fury as she looked from the bag in Cooper's hand to Annie and then Kate.

"I forgot my notebook," Sasha said as she stepped forward and grabbed the bag from Cooper. No one made a move to take it back from her. "I didn't think I'd find my three best friends going through my locker looking for stuff," she added.

"We can explain," Annie said.

"So start explaining," said Sasha.

"It's just that—" Kate began, stopping when she didn't know how to proceed. "Friday night—"

"We followed you on Saturday," Cooper said, saving Kate from having to say anything else. "We saw you talk to that girl at the park. We assumed—"

"You assumed that I must have had something to do with the break-in," Sasha said, finishing the thought for her. She looked down. When she looked up some of the anger had faded from her eyes. "I guess that makes sense," she said. "Although I wish you had just asked me instead of following me."

Kate, Annie, and Cooper looked at each other sheepishly.

"Just so you know, I didn't have anything to do with the robbery," Sasha said.

"Then how—" asked Cooper, nodding at the bag.

"And who—" Annie began simultaneously. They both stopped, their questions unfinished, and looked at Sasha.

Sasha looked at her friends. She pulled her backpack from her locker, put the bag of jewelry and money into it, and shut the locker again.

"Come on," she said. "There's someone I think you guys should meet."

CHAPTER 7

"I can't believe we're skipping school," said Annie as Sasha led her, Kate, and Cooper into the park. She'd been repeating variations of the same phrase ever since Sasha had convinced them to skip their last two periods and come with her. Cooper had had no reservations at all about simply walking out of school, but Kate and Annie had been a little more hesitant. Finally, though, their curiosity had won out and they'd followed along behind the others, nervously waiting for a teacher or other authority figure to confront them. No one had, however, and the girls had taken the bus downtown to the park without incident.

Now they were walking back toward the fountain where they'd seen Sasha talking to the unfamiliar girl. But instead of stopping there, Sasha led them past it and into a stand of trees that sat about a hundred yards away from the fountain area. She walked in among them, making sure the others were following, and walked down a narrow footpath.

"Where does this go?" Cooper asked as she pushed aside the branches of an overgrown tree to keep from being hit in the face by them.

"You'll see in a minute," Sasha replied cryptically.

The path led deeper into the woods. It clearly hadn't been heavily trafficked in a long time, as the growth on either side was threatening to obscure it completely and the bits and pieces of trash that littered its length had been dropped there long ago and were now faded and disintegrated.

They turned a corner, emerging from the trees, and came to a stop in a clearing of sorts. It was a wide, grassy circle perhaps a hundred feet across. In the center of it sat what could easily have been mistaken for a dilapidated Greek temple, complete with pillars on all four sides and a series of marble steps going up to an open doorway in the front. One of the columns had fallen or been knocked down, graffiti covered the sides, and vines were consuming a portion of the roof, but still it was impressive.

"How did this get here?" Annie asked, staring at the building.

"Don't get too excited," Sasha replied. "It's just a shell. It was built to hide a water pump."

The girls approached the building and walked up the steps. Sasha entered the darkened doorway. When the others hesitated, she turned and put her hands on her hips. "It's okay," she said. "Trust me."

"I don't know who we're meeting in here, but I

don't like it," said Annie as she, Kate, and Cooper followed Sasha inside.

Just as Sasha had said, the inside of the building was plain old cinderblock. Empty beer cans, broken bottles, cigarette butts, and food wrappers were scattered around, and the smell was less than refreshing.

"Kids use this place to party in," said Sasha, picking her way through the debris.

"Apparently," Kate said, sniffing and looking at the floor with distaste.

"And how did you know about it?" asked Cooper.

"From my runaway days," replied Sasha. "I met some kids who were living here. They let me stay with them for a week or so until I went to the shelter."

Annie, Cooper, and Kate exchanged glances. None of them could believe that their friend had actually stayed in such a place. It was another reminder to them that there was a lot they didn't know about Sasha. *And a lot we probably don't want to know*, thought Annie.

Sasha led them through the big main room to another door. There they saw a set of stairs going down into the earth.

"We're going down there?" asked Kate nervously.

"It's okay," Sasha told her. "There's nothing dangerous down there."

She walked down the stairs with the others

behind her. They were surprised to see that the stairway was illuminated by dirty lightbulbs strung on a cord that ran overhead. Still, they didn't look too closely at the stained walls—or at the things that crunched beneath their feet as they stepped.

"This place is a really great hideout," Sasha told them as they walked. "Some of the street kids started a rumor that it's haunted, and that keeps most of the people away."

"That's not such a hard story to believe," commented Cooper as she brushed a spiderweb out of her hair and saw its former occupant scurry across the wall.

They were in a short hallway, and up ahead they could see flickering light. "That's the pump room," explained Sasha.

Suddenly a shadow detached from the wall and loomed in front of them. "What are you doing here?" said a threatening voice.

Annie gave a shriek, causing Kate to do the same, while Cooper immediately moved to stand beside Sasha, her fists raised.

"It's okay," Sasha said, putting her hand up to keep Cooper from doing anything. Then she looked at the person still hiding in the shadows. "Mallory, it's me. These are my friends."

"Why did you bring them here?" said the voice again. It sounded anxious and edgy, as if the speaker sensed some kind of threat.

"I think it's time you met them," Sasha said.

"Let's go back there and talk."

The figure stepped forward into the grimy light, and the girls saw that it was the strange girl Sasha had spoken to on Saturday. She looked even dirtier than she had in the sunlight, and she was still wearing her dark glasses, even though Kate, Cooper, and Annie were having a difficult time finding their way with the help of the lightbulbs.

The girl didn't say anything, but she turned and walked away. Every couple of steps she turned and glanced quickly at them, as if she was trying to catch them sneaking up on her. Sasha stayed several feet back from her and motioned for the others to do the same. They weren't sure why she was treating the girl so carefully, but they followed her lead and hung back.

When they entered the room at the end of the hall the girl turned to face them. "Okay," she said, addressing Sasha. "Introduce us."

"This is Kate, Annie, and Cooper," sad Sasha, indicating each of her friends in turn. "They're my best friends. They're the ones who helped me when I was on the streets." She looked at her friends and then nodded toward the girl. "This is Mallory," she said.

"And just who is Mallory?" asked Cooper, an edge to her voice.

"Nice to meet you, too," Mallory said angrily. She looked at Cooper defiantly, her hands thrust into her pockets.

"Mallory and I go way back," Sasha told them.

"We met when I first ran away from home. She's like a sister to me."

"You still haven't told me why you brought them here," said Mallory, not sounding very sister-like. "This could blow everything."

"I brought them here because I think they can help," Sasha said gently.

Mallory snorted. "I don't need any help," she said. "I was doing fine on my own."

"You call breaking into my friends' store doing fine?" Sasha shot back. She turned to the others, who were looking at Mallory with various degrees of surprise and anger.

"*You* broke into Crones' Circle?" Cooper asked.

Mallory didn't say anything, but Sasha nodded. "She needed money," she said. "She'd seen us go in there. She didn't know."

"Didn't know what?" Cooper said, her voice rising. "Didn't know that taking things that belong to other people is wrong? Didn't know that breaking a window and doing your shopping in the middle of the night is wrong? What part of that didn't she know?"

"Hey," Mallory said, advancing on Cooper. "I don't need this from you. Who the hell are you, anyway? You're all rich kids whose mommies and daddies buy them everything they want. So why don't you just get off my case?"

She was right in Cooper's face, pointing a finger and speaking loudly. Cooper's hands were balled at her sides, as if any second she was going to haul off and send Mallory flying backward. The silence in the room was suffocating as the two of them faced one another. Then Cooper's hands relaxed and she looked at Sasha.

"Maybe your friend here is right," she said, clearly trying to control her temper. "Maybe she doesn't need our help. But I'll tell you one thing—she'd better return everything she took from that store."

"Don't worry," Sasha said. "I've got all of it. Well, most of it," she said. "That's what's in the bag that you found in my locker."

"I couldn't get anything for that junk jewelry anyway," Mallory said. "Keep it."

"How big of you," snapped Cooper. "Come on," she said to the others, "let's get out of here."

"Cooper," Sasha said. Her voice was soft, almost pleading.

Cooper turned to look at her. "Please," Sasha said.

"Let her go," Mallory said, her voice dripping with derision. "And don't go bringing your friends around here anymore. I don't need anyone else knowing where I am."

Cooper looked at Mallory, then at Sasha. "I'm out of here," she said.

She stormed down the hallway. After a moment Kate and Annie followed her, with Sasha bringing up the rear.

"You guys," she said. "Wait. We can't just leave."

"Why not?" asked Cooper as she continued to walk.

They went back up the stairs and emerged into the slightly less hazy atmosphere of the main room. Cooper walked through it quickly, going out into the afternoon sun. She stood on the steps of the building and waited for the others to join her. When they did, they all stood together awkwardly, nobody saying anything.

"I know this looks bad," Sasha said finally.

"*Looks* bad?" Cooper retorted. "It *is* bad. That girl broke into Crones' Circle and stole all that stuff."

"I'm giving it back," Sasha said pleadingly. "I was going to leave it in a bag outside the store tonight."

"Oh, so you're not even going to tell them who did it?" Cooper snapped. "You're just going to let her keep living here at the Beecher Falls Hilton and bring her food?"

She and Sasha glared at each other for a moment. Then Sasha said quietly, "She's in trouble."

Cooper snorted. "I'll say," she said. "Pretty big trouble once the police find out what she did."

"I thought I could trust you," Sasha said, sounding hurt. "That's why I brought you here. Not to prove to you that I didn't steal that stuff. I thought maybe we could do something for Mallory." She paused. "The way you did something for me," she added.

Cooper looked away. "She doesn't want our help," she said.

"Neither did I when you first offered it," Sasha said. "It's because she's scared."

"Why is she here?" Annie asked when nobody else spoke. "How did she find you?"

"I told her I was coming here," explained Sasha. "We hung out together in L.A. I wanted her to come, but she was all wrapped up in this guy, so I came by myself."

"So why is she here now?" asked Kate.

Sasha took a deep breath. "Because of that guy," she answered. "He's kind of after her."

"Why?" said Annie.

"Because she knows too much about him," Sasha continued. She hesitated. "When you live on the street you do some things you aren't really proud of," she said softly. "Mallory isn't a bad person; she's just had a really rough time."

"What is it she knows about this guy?" asked Cooper, sounding a little less angry than she had earlier.

"I don't know the details," Sasha replied. "I didn't ask and she didn't tell me. All she said was that she needs to stay out of his way for a while."

"Does he know where she is?" Kate inquired.

Sasha shrugged. "He's in tight with the street community," she said. "It's possible word has gotten out that Mallory came this way. She doesn't know. She's only been gone a week or so. She hung around downtown until she saw me on the street one day. I couldn't believe it when she came up to me. I thought she was just another panhandler, and I started to give her some change." She smiled and laughed slightly. "It's weird thinking that I used to *be* her before I met you guys. When I realized who she was, it all came back to me—the begging, the hunger, the fear. So when she asked me to help her, I had to say yes."

"So you've been bringing her food," said Annie.

Sasha nodded. "I tried to get her to come home with me, but she's too scared still. She won't go to a shelter or anything like that. She thinks she's better off trying to take care of herself."

"I don't get it," said Kate. "Why wouldn't she want to be somewhere where she was protected?"

"It's hard to explain," said Sasha. "A lot of kids on the streets are there because they were thrown around by the system that was supposed to help them. They don't trust anyone. Even though it seems weird to outsiders, they'd rather be the only ones responsible for themselves than risk getting hurt by asking for help. I know how that feels."

"Okay," Cooper said. "What can we do for her?"

Sasha hesitated. "You can start by not telling Sophia or anyone else who really broke into the store," she said.

"Fine," said Cooper after a minute. "As long as whatever she took goes back, we won't say anything. Agreed?" She looked at Kate and Annie, who nodded.

"Agreed," they said in unison.

"What else?" asked Cooper. "Are you just going

to keep bringing her food?"

Sasha nodded. "There's not much else I can do right now," she answered. "I'm hoping that as she starts to trust me more she'll agree to come home with me or something. But right now food is about the best I can do."

"I can probably help with that," said Kate. "My mother brings a lot of leftovers home from her catering jobs. I can get some of that."

"Thanks," said Sasha. "I appreciate it."

"I can make some stuff," Annie said. "I'm always cooking anyway, so nobody will notice."

Sasha nodded. Then she looked at Cooper.

"Don't expect me to cook," said Cooper. "I can't even make soup. But I'll help you bring it down here, how's that?"

"Perfect," Sasha replied. "Thanks, guys. I can't tell you how much this means to me. And to Mallory," she added. "Even if she can't admit it yet."

The four friends left the clearing and walked back down the path, not speaking. When they emerged again into the area around the fountain, they stopped. It felt like being in a totally different world, one with clean, fresh air and a bright, shining sun overhead.

"I feel like Persephone," remarked Kate. "It's like we went down into the underworld and came back again."

"Except that not all of us got to leave," said Sasha.

"Well, let's hope she won't be there much longer," said Annie, putting her arm around her friend. "After all, spring is coming, right? That's when Persephone returned home to her mother."

Sasha looked around at the trees, which were still wrapped in their bare winter skins. "It can't come soon enough," she said sadly.

CHAPTER 8

Kate took one of the heart-shaped cookies from the plate that Meg was carrying around and looked at it. It was a sugar cookie, delicately iced with pretty pink frosting, and written across it in red icing were the words BITE ME.

"What does yours say?" Kate asked Sasha.

Sasha held up her cookie. She had already taken a nibble, so that the cookie now read LOVE ME NO.

"It said 'Love Me Not,'" Sasha explained, noting Kate's puzzled expression.

"Ah," said Kate, nodding. She turned to Cooper, who had just joined them. "Nice work on the cookies."

"Who said I had anything to do with it?" replied Cooper defensively.

"Who else would think of anti-Valentine cookies?" Kate asked.

"They *are* pretty cool, aren't they?" said Cooper, raising her eyebrows and smiling. "I always hated those little candy hearts with the dumb sayings, so I thought I'd make my own statement."

"Out of all of us, shouldn't you be the one who *is* celebrating Valentine's Day?" Sasha asked Cooper. "Where's your boyfriend?"

"He and Schroedinger's Cat are playing some dance over at the college," answered Cooper. "He's taking me out later this week. We didn't want to make it look like we were buying into all of this Hallmark made-up holiday stuff."

"Then all of this bitterness is just to make us nondating losers feel better, is that it?" Sasha said.

"Pretty much," said Cooper. "Is it working?"

They were standing in the living room of Annie's house, waiting for everyone to arrive. In addition to the four of them, they had invited Tara, Jessica, and Jane to get together for dinner and fun—none of it involving boys, cards, or flowers. Their weekly Wicca study group had been canceled for the night so that the participants could indulge in whatever Valentine's Day activities they had planned, and the girls had decided to protest the whole holiday. "Romance is *strictly* off-limits," Annie had told everyone.

The doorbell rang and Kate went to answer it. Standing on the doorstep was Jane. She was dressed totally in black, and she was carrying a bag.

"I got the videos," she said, holding up the sack.

"Nothing but downers. My rule was: Someone has to die horribly."

"You rock," said Kate. "Come on in."

As Jane was greeting everyone the bell rang again. This time it was Tara and Jessica. They greeted Kate with big hugs. "We brought the music," Tara announced as the two of them swept into the house. "And not a happy love song in the bunch."

Tara headed straight for the CD player and started putting in discs. Moments later the sound of a woman's plaintive voice emerged from the speakers.

"It's Billie Holiday," she said. "Old jazz singer. *Very* tragic. All her songs were about how awful her boyfriends were. It's perfect."

As Billie Holiday sang, the girls joined Annie in the kitchen, where pots and pans covered every available surface and the room was filled with steam.

"I hope everybody likes pasta," she said. "We're having penne with goat cheese, sun-dried tomatoes, and pine nuts. Also, pear, blue cheese, and toasted walnut salad. And there's lemon meringue pie for dessert."

"Who died and made you Martha Stewart?" Jane asked as she helped Annie drain the pasta.

"It's all really easy," said Annie confidentially. "I just put out lots of pans to make it look like it was a big deal."

As the girls all helped carry bowls and plates and silverware to the table, Annie stopped Sasha. "I saved some for Mallory," she whispered. "We can take it to her tomorrow."

Sasha laughed. "I'm sure she's been *dying* for pear, blue cheese, and toasted walnut salad," she said jokingly. "Thanks."

When the food was all on the table, everyone pulled up chairs and sat down. As they were getting settled, Annie's aunt walked in. When the girls saw how dressed up she was they whistled and clapped. Aunt Sarah did a turn for them, showing off the gorgeous red dress she was wearing.

"Got a hot date?" Cooper asked her.

"As a matter of fact, I do," Sarah answered. "I'm picking up my honey at the airport and we're going out to dinner. He decided to surprise me with a little visit."

"Actually, you don't even have to pick me up at the airport."

Everyone turned to see Grayson Dunning standing in the doorway of the kitchen. "Sorry to sneak up on everyone like this," he said. "The door was unlocked so I let myself in."

Aunt Sarah went over and gave him a hug and a kiss. "I thought you weren't coming in until eight," she said happily.

"We got an earlier flight," Mr. Dunning said.

"We?" Annie said hopefully.

"Thanks for leaving me with the bags," said a

voice from the hallway. A moment later Becka's face appeared. Annie squealed with delight and jumped up. Seconds later the two girls were hugging one another.

"This is so cool," said Annie. "I had no idea."

"I didn't either," Becka said. "Dad surprised me at the last minute."

"You're just in time for dinner," Annie told her.

"And *you're* just in time to go out for dinner," Aunt Sarah told Mr. Dunning. She turned to the girls. "Don't wait up," she said, winking.

"Okay, but don't do anything I wouldn't do," Meg said sternly. Everyone looked at her and broke out in laughter. "What," Meg said seriously, "is so funny?"

Mr. Dunning and Aunt Sarah left and the girls returned to their dinner. After making a place for Becka in between Jane and Kate, glasses were filled and plates were piled with food. For the next few minutes the only sounds were those of forks clicking and people asking for things to be passed.

"This is so much better than going to some stupid dance," said Tara as she slurped a piece of penne into her mouth.

"Tell me about it," said Jessica. "No having to get all dressed up in a stupid dress and shoes that pinch."

"No mystery punch and packaged cookies," added Kate.

"No terrible band playing 'My Heart Will Go On,'" said Cooper.

"No pink streamers and clouds made out of cotton," mused Jane.

"No ditzy girls wearing too much hair spray," Becka said.

"No watching Sherrie act like the queen of the universe," opined Annie.

"And no stupid boys who can't kiss," said Meg decidedly.

Everyone looked at her. "And since when do you know all about kissing?" Annie demanded to know.

Meg blushed. "I don't know *all* about it," she said. "Maybe a little." She looked at everyone staring at her. "Okay, so Jimmy Poling kissed me after school last week."

The older girls oohed and aahed, making Meg turn red. "I didn't say I *liked* it," she said huffily.

"We'll talk later," Annie told her little sister. "Right now, who wants more penne?"

For the next hour they talked, ate, and laughed, not worrying about how much they ate or how they looked. They talked about bad dates and boyfriends who did stupid things. And when they were done with dinner they piled the dishes in the sink and went into the living room to watch movies.

"This is the coolest Valentine's Day I've ever had," Kate said as they settled onto the couch and on the floor. "You guys are the best date ever."

"I agree," Becka said. "But will you call us tomorrow, or will you be like all the rest of them?"

"Time for pie," said Annie, coming in with a tray loaded with plates, forks, and a big, cold lemon pie whose meringue covered the top like ocean waves on a windy day.

Once the pie was dished out they started the first movie. When it was over they took a break so people could visit the bathroom and get seconds on pie. While the girls were running around, Cooper stood up, stretched, and said, "I hate to be the one to leave first, but I've got to get home."

"Really?" Kate asked. "You can't stay?"

"I want to make sure everything is okay," answered Cooper. She turned to Annie. "But this was really great. It almost makes me want to dump T.J." She looked thoughtful. "But not quite."

She waved good-bye to everyone else, turned to Jane and said "I'll call you tomorrow," and then left. Ten minutes later she was walking in the door of her own house.

"Hey," she called out. "I'm home."

To her surprise she heard her mother call back, "I'm in the living room. Come in here."

She's not drunk, Cooper thought excitedly as she took off her coat and went to see her mother.

Mrs. Rivers was sitting in one of the armchairs. She seemed to be completely sober, or at least mostly. She did have a glass in her hand, but it was almost full, and a quick glance at the bottle on the table beside her showed that barely any of it had been drunk. Cooper knew, though, that just because this bottle was full it didn't mean that there wasn't an empty bottle—or several—in the kitchen trash can.

"Sit down," Mrs. Rivers said to her daughter. "I want to talk to you."

Cooper sat on the couch and looked at her mother. Mrs. Rivers was looking down at the floor. She didn't say anything for a long time. Then she looked up, and her face was hard, her eyes angry.

"I got a phone call tonight," she said in a clipped voice. "From Mrs. McAllister."

Suddenly Cooper's elation at finding her mother sober faded. T.J.'s mother had called. Cooper had known that she would keep her promise, but she hadn't known when it would happen. She sort of wished she'd had some advance warning. But it was too late now.

"Oh," Cooper said. "What did she want?"

"She asked if I wanted to get together for coffee," Mrs. Rivers answered. "Sometime during the week."

"That would be fun," said Cooper brightly, hoping her enthusiastic response would throw her mother off and prevent the argument Cooper had a feeling was coming.

"I'm sure it would be," said Mrs. Rivers. "For you. Cooper, I don't appreciate being made a fool of."

"I don't know what you mean," Cooper said truthfully.

"I mean having you tell this woman that I have some kind of . . . problem—or whatever it is you told her."

"I didn't—" Cooper began to say.

"Of course you did!" Mrs. Rivers shouted. "You told her *something*. Why else would she call after all this time? You should have heard her voice, Cooper. She felt *sorry* for me. She *pitied* me. I could hear it in every word she said." She stared at her daughter, her mouth twitching. "Do you have any idea how that feels?"

Cooper didn't respond. She looked away from her mother, trying to decide what she should say.

"Do you?" Mrs. Rivers shouted again.

Cooper looked up. Her mother was clutch-ing her glass. Whatever was in it had spilled over onto the wooden floor of the room, where it made a tiny puddle by her foot. More of the drink stained the fabric of the armchair, and Cooper saw drops of it on the ring that circled her mother's finger.

"No," Cooper said. "I don't know how that feels." She waited until her mother began to look as if she'd won the fight, then added, "But I do know how it feels to watch somebody I care about turn into somebody I can't even stand to look at."

She stood up and started to leave the room, but stopped when she heard her mother say, in the coldest voice Cooper had ever heard her use, "How dare you."

Cooper turned around. Her mother was standing up, facing her. Her arms were stiff at her sides, her fingers curled into her palms.

"How dare you say something like that to me," Mrs. Rivers said. "You have no idea what I'm going through. None at all."

"Maybe I don't," said Cooper. "But there are people who do."

Her mother gave a strangled laugh. "Who?" she said. "People like Mrs. McAllister?"

"Yes," Cooper replied. "People like her. She's a nice lady. She just wants to be your friend."

Mrs. Rivers shook her head. "I don't need friends," she said. "I don't need people feeling sorry for me. And I certainly don't need *you* thinking you know what's best for me. So I'd appreciate it if you'd get out of my life. You and your father both, although he's already done that, hasn't he?"

Cooper bit her lip. There were so many things she wanted to say to her mother at that moment, and none of them were nice. She could feel the rage and anger radiating from her mother like heat from a stove. It nauseated her and it made her want to cry. She couldn't be around it, so she turned and left the room. Grabbing her coat, she ran out of the house, slamming the door behind her.

She stormed over to her car and got in. Then she sat there. While she'd made a dramatic exit, the problem was that she had no idea where she was going. She didn't want to return to Annie's house. She didn't want to go see T.J. She didn't know what she wanted. She just didn't want to be around her mother, not when she was acting so cruel and saying such terrible things.

But how many times did you say things like that to her? she asked herself. *How many times did you get angry and say things you didn't really mean?*

She thought about the question. If she was honest about it, she had to admit that she'd done it many times. Their relationship had always been tempestuous, and more than once Cooper had slammed a door or told her mother she never wanted to see her again. She thought about the time when she was thirteen and they'd fought over some stupid thing. Cooper couldn't even remember what it was. But she remembered telling her mother she hated her and her mother saying, "I'm sure you do, but you only get one mother in life and I'm it."

She leaned her head against the steering wheel. She was running away from the problem, and she hated doing that. She was walking out because things were hard, and her usual methods of dealing with things when they were hard were to either run away or bulldoze through whatever was causing the problem. But she'd learned that those two approaches weren't the only ones—and were seldom even the best ones.

"You need to go back in there," she told herself. "You need to do what she did to you when you were thirteen."

She looked at the door. It was weird how a house could look so normal from the outside— just four walls and a roof—but how inside it could be filled with so much danger. Just thinking about walking through the door made her feel sick to her stomach. But the idea of running away made her feel just as sick.

She got out, shut the car door, and walked back to the house. This time when she went inside she marched straight into the living room. Her mother was once again seated in the chair. Her glass was filled again, and Cooper noticed that the level in the bottle had decreased dramatically.

"Did you come back to tell me something else?" Mrs. Rivers asked, not looking up at her daughter.

"Yeah," Cooper said. "I came back to tell you that you're probably only going to get one daughter in this life, and I'm it. So as long as we're stuck with each other, you're going to listen to what I have to say." She kept talking, afraid that if she stopped she would lose her nerve or her mother would start talking and interrupt her. "You're right that I don't know what you're going through. But you don't know what I'm going through, either. I talked to

Mrs. McAllister because I thought maybe she could help. I didn't know who else to go to. I'm sorry if that made you feel embarrassed. But you have to talk to somebody, because I can't watch you do what you're doing. You're scaring me."

She stopped talking and watched her mother's face. There was no expression on it. She just looked into the glass in her hand. *She didn't hear a word of what I said,* Cooper thought unhappily. She had made her grand speech and her mother wasn't even responding. Cooper wanted to disappear. Having her mother not say anything at all was far worse than having her yell. *At least then I'd know she heard me,* she thought.

"That's it," Cooper said finally. "I'm going to bed." She turned to leave.

"I'm scared, too."

She turned around at the sound of her mother speaking. Tears were falling from her mother's eyes, rolling slowly down her cheeks and falling into her glass.

"I don't know what's happening to me," said Mrs. Rivers. Her shoulders shook as she began to cry harder, and she put her hands up to cover her face, in the process knocking her glass to the floor.

Cooper went to her mother. She knelt down, not caring that the contents of the glass were soaking the knees of her jeans. She took her mother's hands, pulling them away from her face.

Mrs. Rivers looked away, as if looking at Cooper was more than she could bear.

"It's okay," said Cooper. "It will be okay." *I don't know how*, she told herself as she watched her mother cry and felt the roles they'd played all their lives reversing, *but it will be okay*.

CHAPTER 9

"You guys have the strangest friends," said Becka as she and Annie made their way to the park the next day. She and her father were staying until the weekend, and Annie's aunt had given Annie permission to miss a day of school so that she and Becka could spend some time together. Annie had told Becka about Mallory and asked her to help take some things to the girl.

"I don't know if she'll even accept this stuff," Annie said as she and Becka walked through the park. "She's so defensive. It's probably best if we just leave it inside with a note. That way she doesn't have to act all grateful or anything."

Becka was carrying two shopping bags filled with leftovers that Annie had prepared. In addition to the food from the party, she had made some lasagna and some cookies. She'd also bought some canned stuff at the supermarket and added it to the bags along with a can opener. While Becka carried the food, Annie was carrying bags filled with clothes that she'd culled from her closet. She'd also found an old sleeping bag, which she was now carrying under her arm as she and Becka walked toward Mallory's hiding place.

The park was slightly more populated than it had been the last time the girls had come through, mostly with kids who should have been in school but weren't. The area around the fountain was busy with skateboarders, who were using its smooth sides to practice sliding their boards along the rim. They mostly ignored Annie and Becka after giving them perfunctory glances to ensure that the girls weren't there to tell them to stop what they were doing.

"Hey, you got any smokes?"

Annie and Becka stopped and looked to see who had called to them. A guy was sitting on the edge of the fountain, looking at them. He seemed to be a little older than they were. His brown hair was cut very short, and he had a handsome face with oddly light blue eyes. He was dressed in an old leather jacket, jeans, and black motorcycle boots. When they looked at him he smiled crookedly. "Got any smokes?" he repeated.

Annie shook her head. "Sorry," she said. "We don't smoke."

"You're smart," the guy said. "It's a bad habit."

Annie and Becka started to walk away but the guy called out to them again. "Going camping?"

Becka turned her head. "We're launching an

expedition to find Atlantis," she said, feigning seriousness. "We hear the entrance is around here somewhere."

"Becka," Annie said under her breath. "Come on."

"He's just flirting," Becka said back. "Have a little fun. Besides, he's sort of cute."

Annie rolled her eyes, but she also gave her friend a small smile. She was enjoying being with Becka, and one of the things she liked most was her friend's sense of adventure. *What's the harm in doing a little flirting?* she asked herself.

The guy had come over to where the girls were standing. He walked in an easygoing way, as if he had all the time in the world and nowhere in particular to go. When he stopped he stood with his hands in the pockets of his jeans, leaning his weight on one leg so that he looked like he was waiting casually for a bus to come along.

"An expedition, huh?" he said, nodding.

"That's right," Becka replied. "You can't be too prepared, you know."

The guy laughed. "I hear you," he said. "But I'd be careful around here if I were you. I hear a lot of runaway kids hang out in this place."

"Really?" Becka said, as if the information truly shocked her. "I had no idea."

The guy nodded. "That's the word on the street," he said, as if imparting very valuable information to them for free.

"And just what are *you* doing here?" Becka asked him.

The guy shrugged. "You know," he said. "Just hanging out. Hoping some pretty girls might have a cigarette I could bum."

"I see," Becka said. "Well, no cigarettes here. But maybe something better will come along."

She picked up her bags and nodded at Annie. "Come on," she said. "We've got some exploring to do."

Annie followed as Becka looked at the guy, said, "See you later," and continued walking.

"I hope so," the guy called after them. "And remember what I said; be careful."

"I can't believe you talked to him like that," Annie said as she and Becka made their way around the side of the fountain and headed for the trees beyond it.

"He's just a guy," Becka replied. "Guys are easy to talk to. You just have to think of them as big, stupid dogs who want you to like them. Then it's easy."

"With me it's more like I'm afraid they're going to bite me," Annie said. "I've never been very good at the whole talking-to-guys thing."

"We'll work on that when we're living together," Becka told her. It was the first time either of them had mentioned the impending merging of their families since Becka's arrival.

"Still no word from your dad about where, huh?" Annie asked. They had reached the path and

Annie stopped, looking around to make sure no one was watching them. Then she stepped through the branches of the trees with Becka following behind her.

"Not a thing," said Becka. "I tried to harass him into talking about it on the plane ride here, but he pretended to be really into the in-flight magazine and just grunted at me."

"I guess we'll find out when we find out," remarked Annie. "But it would be nice to know."

They walked in silence until they reached the clearing. Becka whistled when she saw the fake temple, then whistled again for a different reason when they stepped inside it and she saw the mess. "She lives in this?" she asked Annie.

Annie set down her bags. "This is the *nice* part," she told Becka. "You don't even want to know about the rest of it."

"In that case, I'm all for leaving the stuff here and splitting," Becka said.

"I agree," said Annie. She took out a piece of paper and a pen from the backpack she was wearing. "Let me just leave Mallory a note so she knows this stuff is for her."

"You don't have to do that."

Annie looked up and saw Mallory watching her from the doorway leading to the stairs. She wasn't wearing her sunglasses this time, and Annie saw that she had a pretty, sad face. She looked tired.

"I meant that you don't have to leave a note,"

Mallory said, stepping out of the shadows. "The stuff you can leave."

"Oh," said Annie, unsure of what to say to the girl who had basically chased them all out of her hideout on Monday.

Mallory looked at Becka. "Another one?" she asked. "What, have you guys got a club or something?"

"This is my friend Becka," Annie said.

"Hey," Becka said to Mallory. "Cool fort. But you need a sign outside saying 'No Boys Allowed' if you want it to be perfect."

Annie watched Mallory to see how she would react. She couldn't believe that Becka was acting so nonchalant about the situation. She was talking to Mallory the same way she'd talked to the guy at the fountain, and once again Annie was reminded of how shy she herself usually was.

Mallory studied Becka for a minute without saying anything. Then she looked at Annie. "I like this one," she said. "She's a lot better than that loudmouth you had with you last time."

"She means Cooper," Annie explained to Becka, who suppressed a smile.

"Thanks for the food," said Mallory, glancing into the bags Annie had left for her. She reached into one of the bags and pulled out a shirt that Annie had brought. It was an old flannel one, green and blue, that Annie had worn until she was sick of it. Mallory immediately put it on, pushing her hair back so that it fell over her shoulders. Looking at her, Annie saw herself standing there, and for a moment she imagined what it would be like if she were living the way Mallory was. Suddenly she saw Mallory totally differently than she had only two days ago. She wasn't mean; she was scared. She wasn't refusing their help; she was trying to maintain some of her pride.

"It looks good on you," Annie told her.

Mallory didn't say anything, but she nodded. "Thanks again," she said, picking up the bags and turning to leave.

"We'll come back tomorrow, if you want," Annie said hurriedly.

"If you want," said Mallory as she disappeared back into the darkness.

Annie looked at Becka and the two of them left. When they were away from the building Annie said, "I can't even imagine living like that."

"I can't either," replied Becka. "She seems nice."

Nice. It wasn't a word Annie would ever think of to describe Mallory. She thought about how nasty the girl had been to them the first time they'd met. Then she thought about how sad she'd looked putting on the old flannel shirt, like any other teenage girl who wanted to feel good. She wasn't any different, really, from Annie and her friends. She'd just had some bad luck.

As they walked back along the path through the trees, Annie thought about Mallory and how her life had turned out. The month before, they had been studying astrology in their weekly Wicca study group. That's how Annie had found out about the existence of the older sister she'd never known about. At the time, Annie had thought a lot about the notion that peoples' destinies were already written for them based on the alignments of the stars and planets at the time of their birth. She'd hated the notion, because it made her feel trapped by circumstances over which she had no control. She thought about that again now as she pondered Mallory's situation. Was she living the life she was because of some predestined path she was walking? Or was everything a result of choices Mallory had made, purely her own doing? Annie didn't know, just as she still didn't really understand why events in her life had played out the way they had.

"Can I ask you something really personal?" she inquired of Becka.

"Hey, we're going to be sharing parental figures and possibly a bathroom," Becka answered. "It doesn't get a lot more personal than that. Ask away."

"Do you think there was a reason for your mother's death?" said Annie. She held her breath, hoping that Becka had meant what she'd said about being free to ask anything.

Becka was quiet for a minute or two as they continued walking. Annie wondered if she was thinking about her mother, who had drowned shortly after Becka was born.

"I know what you're asking," Becka said finally. "And I don't know if I have an answer. I'd like to *think* that there was a reason for it, but to be honest I haven't found one yet, and I've been thinking for a long time."

"Do you think about how your life might be different if she hadn't died?" Annie asked her.

"I probably wouldn't be talking to you right now, for one thing," Becka said. "And my dad and your aunt wouldn't be off picking out china patterns or whatever it is they're doing today."

"I know all that," Annie said. "I mean, do you think you would be a different person?"

"I can't answer that," said Becka. "This is the life I've got. I don't know how it might have been different. Can I ask why you're asking?"

"I was just thinking about how sometimes everything seems like a total accident," said Annie. "But then other times it's like I can see these patterns happening, making sense of everything. Only usually when I start thinking that maybe there is a pattern or a plan or whatever something happens to totally blow that theory apart."

"My dad says writing books is sort of like that," Becka told her. "Sometimes he'll start off with this really great idea, and he'll plan every single step of the book. Then he starts writing and the characters decide to do something else that has nothing to do with his plan."

"What does he do then?" Annie asked.

Becka laughed. "Usually he sits around watching a lot of really bad television until he's ready to write again," she said. "Then he gets back to it. He says that almost every single time he has no idea why a book is turning out the way it is and he thinks he's made a mistake and should start over, there comes this point where he suddenly sees that everything he's been writing—all the weird things the characters have been saying and doing—is for a reason. He just didn't know what the reason was until the story was almost finished. Then he sees it, and he's able to finish the book because he sees the end of the story."

"That makes it sound like the story belongs to the characters, and he's just kind of telling it," Annie remarked.

"I think that is how it is a lot of the time," Becka told her. "He always says that the trick to writing is to come up with really interesting characters and then let them live their lives."

Annie thought about this as they came to the end of the path. Were Grayson Dunning's characters living out lives that had been predestined for them when he created them? Was he like some big god, creating people and then watching them do whatever it was they had to do, and writing about it? Were she and all her friends doing the same thing, living out lives that had been selected for them by someone else? These weren't new questions for her, but she was thinking about them in a new way.

They emerged from the path and walked back

toward the fountain. The skateboarders were still there. They'd set up a jump using an old board and some milk crates, and they were taking turns riding up it and launching themselves into the air. They looked like big, awkward birds when they left the ramp, their long arms flailing as they tried to maintain control over their boards. Then they landed, sometimes falling and sometimes triumphantly raising their hands in the air as their friends cheered. But even when they fell they had smiles on their faces, smiles filled with the thrill of freedom and—for a brief moment—flying.

But are they really free? Annie wondered.

"That must have been one tough expedition," said a voice. "You lost all your gear."

It was the guy from the fountain again. He was walking beside them. He'd found a cigarette somewhere and was smoking it, holding it in the corner of his mouth while he talked. The smoke trickled out and swirled around his head like bugs around an electric light.

"We got hungry," Becka told him. "It was a long walk."

"Did you find what you were looking for?" the guy asked her.

"Maybe," responded Becka. "Maybe not."

The guy nodded. "Well, if you're all done playing Lara Croft, maybe you can help me out."

"Sorry," Annie said. "We told you—we don't smoke."

"It's not cigarettes I'm after," said the guy. He reached into his back pocket and pulled out a crumpled piece of paper. He unfolded it, smoothed it out, and held it up. "I'm looking for this girl."

On the paper was a rough sketch of Mallory. Annie was shocked to see it.

"This is my sister," the guy said. "Her name is Mallory. She ran away from home a little over a year ago. Followed some guy. We've been looking for her ever since."

Annie looked from the sketch to the guy's face. She remembered that Sasha had told them Mallory was running away from a guy who wanted to hurt her. Was this him? Or was he someone who wanted to help her?

"My name is Derek Lowell," the guy told her, smiling sadly. "I've been tracking her from town to town. I know she came here about ten days ago, but that's where the trail ends. No one has seen her." He paused, looking away. When he looked back he had a sad expression on his face. "Mom really misses her," he said. "We all miss her."

Annie glanced at Becka, who gave her a guarded expression. There was something about Derek that Annie just didn't trust. He seemed nice enough, but his appearance in Beecher Falls seemed too coincidental. Maybe he was Mallory's brother, but there was no way to know for sure.

"I haven't seen anyone who looks like that," said Annie, pretending to study the sketch again.

"How about you?" Derek asked Becka.

"I'm just visiting," she answered, giving him a big smile. "Just came for a little adventure, and then I'm going back to San Francisco."

Derek folded the paper and put it back in his pocket. He nodded at them both. "Thanks for taking a look," he said. "I appreciate it."

"I hope you find her," Annie said. "She looks pretty."

"She used to be," said Derek. "I haven't seen her in a long time, so I don't know what she looks like now."

"Well, good luck," said Annie.

She and Becka walked off. As soon as they were out of earshot Annie said, "Do you believe him?"

"No," Becka said. "I don't know why, but I don't."

"Me neither," Annie said. "I think we need to tell the others."

"What about Mallory?" asked Becka. "Shouldn't we warn her? I mean, if it *is* her brother, she would want to know, right? And if it's this other guy, she would definitely want to know."

Annie nodded. "But we can't do it right now," she said. "He's going to keep hanging around. If we head back to the pump house, he's going to know something is up. We'll have to do it later tonight, when he's gone."

"I hope Mallory stays out of sight until then," said Becka.

"I think she will," Annie replied. "She has food, and she's not stupid. But just in case, we should tell Sasha, Kate, and Cooper right away. He hasn't seen them yet, so maybe they can come down and keep an eye on him."

They went back to Annie's house as quickly as they could. It was almost three, and Annie wanted to catch the others as soon as possible. She would leave messages at their houses telling them to call her.

But when she and Becka walked in the door, they were greeted by the sight of Mr. Dunning and Aunt Sarah standing in the foyer, kissing.

"Oh, hey," Mr. Dunning said. "There you are." He and Annie's aunt looked slightly embarrassed at having been caught kissing.

"Hi," Annie said quickly, trying to rush by them to get to the phone. But Mr. Dunning stopped her.

"Not so fast," he said. "We have something to talk to you guys about."

"We already know," Becka said, trying to hurry things along. "You're getting married."

Mr. Dunning looked at Aunt Sarah. "It's not that," he said. He looked back at the girls. "We've decided where we're going to live."

the police search the grounds for Kendall riders we were something in the distance correspond the hides while we were done and door did the kill Duke we spread our cloth the sharing that of the gold gun bottles of sheets

CHAPTER 10

Kate wanted to kill Sherrie. Given the opportunity, she might even have done it. At the very least she would have given Sherrie a piece of her mind. *It's a good thing for her she isn't around*, Kate thought as she walked home, fuming.

She'd gone into the science lab at the end of the day to take a look at the seed trays and to make some notes about the temperature and other conditions they were growing under. Tuesday had been Sherrie's day to check on them, and this was the first chance Kate had had to look at the seeds since planting them on Monday.

But when she'd pulled the seed trays out, she'd discovered that Sherrie had done them backwards. The pots that were supposed to be well watered were dry as a bone, and the ones that were supposed to receive minimal watering looked as if a hurricane had passed through sometime in the forty-eight hours since their planting. Similarly, the seeds that were supposed to be happily sunning themselves beneath the grow light Kate had rigged up were languishing in the darkest corner of the room, while the ones that had been destined for shade were spread out under the glowing suns of the lights like bathers on a beach.

Kate had been forced to dump out the dirt and the seeds and start all over again. Repotting the twenty-four pots had taken her all period. *Although it went much faster than when Sherrie "helped,"* thought Kate as she walked briskly toward her house. Still, it left them two days behind in their experiment *and* it had made her late leaving. She hadn't been able to catch a ride with Cooper and Sasha, and now she had to walk home alone. To make everything worse, it was getting foggy and cold.

When she finally got home, she was looking forward to taking a long, hot shower, putting on some comfortable sweats, and spending the evening reading. *Maybe I'll finally get to look at that book about Ostara rituals Sophia loaned me,* she thought. Sophia had strongly hinted that the girls might be allowed to help plan the Spring Equinox ritual that year. Ostara was the first ritual the girls had ever attended with the coven, and this would be their anniversary of meeting them and hearing about the weekly study group. It was kind of a nostalgic period for everyone, and Kate was looking forward to helping out this year and putting everything she'd learned to use.

When she finally got home and opened the

door, the phone was ringing. She was tempted to ignore it, but out of habit she walked into the kitchen and picked it up.

"Hello?"

"Thank Goddess, you're finally home," said a worried-sounding Annie.

"Where are you?" Kate asked. "You sound funny."

"I'm on a cell phone," Annie replied. "It's my aunt's. Listen, I don't have a lot of time to explain. We're on our way over to get you."

"Get me?" Kate said. "Get me for what?"

"I'll explain everything when we see you," said Annie. "We'll be there in five minutes. Be ready."

Kate hung up and sighed heavily. *So much for a quiet evening at home*, she thought miserably. What did Annie and the others have up their sleeves this time? she wondered. As she went upstairs to quickly change into something warmer, she hoped that whatever they had in mind, it wouldn't be too strenuous. She was so *not* in the mood for running around.

In her room, she removed the clothes she'd worn to school and pulled on a pair of jeans and an old sweatshirt of her father's that she had appropriated because she'd liked the faded blue color. It was much too big on her, but wearing it made her feel good. Besides, it was warm, and she was definitely feeling chilly. She hoped she wasn't coming down with a cold or anything.

She went back downstairs and got her warm

jacket from the hall closet. Pulling it on, she went outside and waited for the others to arrive. They did a minute later, pulling up in Annie's aunt's car. Kate walked over and got into the back, where Cooper and Sasha were already sitting. Becka and Annie were in the front.

"Okay," Kate said, "what's the big plan? It's a school night, so I can't be out too late. Besides, Sherrie totally flaked out on me and I think I'm getting a cold and—" She stopped, noticing the worried looks on the faces of the other girls. "What's wrong?" she asked.

Annie was driving, looking straight ahead with a grim expression. She caught Cooper's eye in the rearview mirror.

"We think Mallory might be in trouble," said Cooper.

"Mallory?" Kate asked. "Why? What happened?" She made a face. "Did someone tell Sophia it was her who broke into the store?" she asked.

"Becka and I took her some food and clothes today," said Annie. "We ran into this guy who asked us if we had seen a missing girl. The picture he was showing around was a drawing of Mallory."

"Who is he?" Kate asked.

"He says he's her brother," Becka told her. "Derek Lowell."

"So, is he?" asked Kate. "I mean, that would be okay, right?"

"Mallory does have a brother named Derek,"

Sasha said. "And yes, it could be him. But it could also be Ray. From what Mallory has told me about her brother, I wouldn't be surprised if he was looking for her. But from what I know about Ray—which is a lot—I'd be even less surprised to find out that he was here. Unfortunately, from the description Annie and Becka gave me, I can't say for sure which of them it is."

"So we're going to go find out," Kate guessed. "Or at least find Mallory and tell her that someone has been asking about her."

"You said that Mallory knows things about Ray that he doesn't want her telling anyone," said Cooper. "Do you think he would hurt her to keep her from talking, or does he just want to scare her?"

Sasha was quiet for a minute. "I don't know what he would do," she said, "but I can tell you from firsthand experience that Ray is not a nice guy."

"The guy we talked to was really kind of charming," Becka told her, clearly trying to be reassuring.

"Oh, Ray can be charming," Sasha replied. "He can be *very* charming."

She stopped talking and looked out the window. Kate wanted to ask her more questions, but she could tell that Sasha didn't want to say any more about Ray and his secrets. Kate suspected that Sasha knew full well why Ray wanted to keep Mallory quiet, but knowing why didn't really matter. All they needed to worry about was finding out who the guy looking for her was and letting her know he was around.

Annie parked the car a few blocks away from the entrance to the park. The girls got out and congregated on the sidewalk to formulate a plan.

"If it's Ray, he knows what I look like," Sasha said, taking charge. "I don't want that to happen before I can talk to Mallory, so I think I should be the one to go look for her. Kate, you come with me. No one should go alone, just in case we run into trouble. Annie, Cooper, and Becka, you guys go check out the area around the fountain. This guy has already seen you. If you run into him, try to stall him long enough for us to get to Mallory and get her out of the pump station."

"Where are we going to take her when we find her?" Cooper asked.

"Back to my house," said Sasha. "I know she won't want to go, but she's got to. I'm not letting her stay out here if Ray is after her. And if it really is her brother after all, then we can bring him to my house later to meet her."

They agreed to meet back at the car in half an hour for a check-in. "If we haven't found Mallory by then, we'll go to Plan B," Sasha informed them.

"What's Plan B?" asked Annie.

"I don't know yet," said Sasha. "I'm hoping Plan A works."

They split up. Cooper, Becka, and Annie headed for the main entrance, while Sasha and Kate went along the side of the park.

"There's a back entrance to the pump station,"

Sasha explained. "It's more overgrown than the other one, but it will keep us out of sight."

They came to a densely wooded area. Sasha walked straight into the trees and disappeared. Following her, Kate was surprised to see that there was a tiny space between some bushes, just thin enough for someone to slip through if she knew it was there. Otherwise, it appeared to be a solid wall of branches.

The two girls picked their way along a path almost totally obscured by vegetation. It was getting dark, and it was difficult to make their way through the gloom. But Sasha pressed on, with Kate right behind her like a shadow, and soon they emerged into the clearing where the old templelike structure stood.

"Are we going to just walk in?" asked Kate nervously. "What if Ray is in there?"

"We don't have a lot of choice," Sasha answered. "Because if Ray is in there, then Mallory is in there, too."

They crept slowly up to the front door and peered inside. The main room seemed to be empty. "Mallory?" Sasha called softly. There was no answer.

The girls went in and walked across the room to the short hallway. Moments later they were going down the filthy stairs. Some of the lightbulbs seemed to have broken, and it was even darker and grungier than it had been the first time they'd descended into the earth. This time, though, they knew what to expect. Even still, Kate shuddered when she saw things skittering away into the darkness as they passed by.

They made their way into the main pump room and looked around. When Kate saw Mallory slumped on the ground, on top of the old sleeping bag Annie had given her earlier, she almost screamed. But Sasha ran to her friend and dropped to her knees.

"Mal?" she said, alarmed.

Mallory's face was covered in blood, as were the clothes she was wearing. It was impossible to see where the blood was coming from, but it covered Sasha's hands as she grabbed her friend and called out her name. The girl's skin was covered in contusions, and one eye was swollen shut.

"Mallory?" Sasha said, sounding frantic. "Mallory?"

Kate held her breath. Was Mallory dead? She couldn't tell. Her body hung, seeming lifeless, in Sasha's arms. She didn't open her eyes or respond to Sasha's voice.

"No," Sasha said. "No. I'm not letting you die." She put her hand on Mallory's neck, feeling for a pulse. "She's alive," she told Kate.

"But not for long."

The girls looked up and saw a young man walk out from behind the broken remains of the pump.

"Ray," Sasha said, her voice filled with a

mixture of fear and hatred. "It is you."

"Sasha," Ray said, grinning broadly. "What a treat. I didn't know Mal was visiting an old friend. She should have told me. Maybe then I wouldn't have had to knock her around. If I remember correctly, you and I have an old score to settle ourselves," Ray said to Sasha. Then he looked at Kate. "Aren't you going to introduce me to your friend?"

Sasha didn't say anything. She was busy wiping the blood from Mallory's face. Kate stared back at Ray, wondering how he could do what he'd done to Mallory and still seem as if he was simply at a party, making conversation.

"That's okay," said Ray smoothly. "You don't have to tell me her name. I'll get it out of one of you, the same way I got what I wanted out of Mal."

Kate looked at Sasha. What were they going to do? They clearly had to get Mallory—and themselves—out of there. But there was only one way out, and Ray was standing right in the middle of it.

"Get out of the way, Ray," Sasha said. Her voice had taken on a flat, emotionless tone, as if she were talking to a dog she didn't much care for. "We're taking Mallory out of here. I suggest you get out, too, because as soon as our friends make their phone call the cops are going to be crawling all over this place."

Ray laughed. "Nice try," he said. "You get an A

for effort. But there are no cops coming. And even if there were, they wouldn't care about some stupid runaway. You should know that, Sasha. After all, they didn't help you when you went to them back in L.A., did they?"

Kate was confused. What was Ray talking about? She looked at Sasha, who suddenly looked very frightened. Ray laughed again. "See, you *do* remember. What makes you think this time will be any different?"

He was walking toward them now, his steps heavy on the concrete floor. Ray edged by Kate and she backed away. He stopped, turning to her and smiling. "Oh, don't worry," he said. "I'll get to you. But first Sasha and I have some unfinished business."

Keeping Kate in his line of vision, he advanced on Sasha with a roar that filled the room. Kate watched it all as if it were happening in slow motion. She saw Ray's arm go up, saw Sasha look up to see what he was doing, saw the look of rage on Ray's face.

She knew that she should do something. She knew that if they had been in a movie, or a TV show, she would suddenly reach down and throw a handful of dirt in Ray's face, blinding him. If she was like those women in the movies, she'd find some way to rush in and save her friend. But she wasn't one of those women. She was just a scared girl who didn't know what to do. All she could do was watch as Ray's hand came down with sickening speed at Sasha's head.

Then she saw Sasha's hand come up. Something gleamed in it, and she saw Sasha slash the air near Ray's wrist. Then she saw Ray grab his arm and clutch it to his chest.

Blood was seeping out from between Ray's fingers where he held his arm. He was howling in pain. Kate looked at Sasha. She was holding a knife in her hand. It was red with Ray's blood. The look on Sasha's face made even Kate frightened of her.

"Kate, help me with Mallory," Sasha called. "Kate!" she said again when Kate didn't move.

Kate snapped out of her trance and ran over to where Mallory lay on the floor, still not moving.

"You're going to have to carry her," Sasha said.

Kate glanced at Ray. He was still doubled over. His shirt was soaked with blood, and he was glaring at Sasha.

"Don't worry about him," Sasha said to Kate. She turned her attention to Ray. "You stay right there until we're gone," she told him. "If you come after us, you're dead."

She didn't wait for a reply from the wounded guy. Kate half carried and half dragged Mallory down the hall, then started up the stairs. Mallory's feet banged on every step, and Kate's arms ached with the effort of holding her up. She could feel her muscles beginning to cramp up.

"I don't think I can do this myself," Kate said when they were halfway up the stairs.

Sasha peered into the darkness, looking for any sign that Ray was following them. Then, reluctantly, she slipped the knife into her pocket. She turned and lifted Mallory's feet.

With the two of them carrying the girl, it was easier to get her up the steps. Soon they were passing through the front room and heading for the door. Outside, Kate could see the grayness of twilight, and her spirits lifted.

Just as they were about to leave the building Ray burst from the shadows and lunged at Sasha with a cry of rage. Kate saw her friend crumple to the ground as Ray grabbed her by the hair and pulled her back. It all happened so quickly that Sasha didn't have time to react, and the end result was that Ray was on top of her, beating her with his good hand while she tried to fight him off.

Kate knew she had to do something. She glanced down and saw a piece of jagged stone, fallen off the crumbling structure. Kate grabbed it and moved toward Ray and Sasha. "Get off her!" she shouted.

Ray looked up and snarled at Kate. He made a move to grab at her, and for a split second Kate was frozen once again. She knew what she had to do, but she couldn't bring herself to do it. *Mother, help me*, she thought, calling on the Goddess for strength.

Then she felt her arms coming down. She felt the stone hit Ray's forehead. The noise of it made her want to scream. Then she realized that she *was* screaming. She also realized that Ray had collapsed on top of Sasha.

"Get him off me!" Sasha was yelling.

Kate dropped the stone, glad to be free of it. She rolled Ray off of Sasha, who scrambled to her feet.

"Is he dead?" Kate asked, staring at Ray's unmoving form.

"Who cares?" said Sasha. "Let's go."

She grabbed Kate, spinning her around and focusing her attention on Mallory. Kate grabbed Mallory under the arms, while Sasha grabbed her feet. Together they carried her outside and down the steps. As they reached the last one they heard a commotion in the bushes, and then Cooper, Annie, and Becka were there.

"Is everyone okay?" asked Annie anxiously.

"We heard screaming," said Becka.

"We're fine," said Sasha. "But Mallory isn't. We need to get her out of here. Now."

The girls helped lift Mallory, and together they carried her as quickly as possible through the trees. The whole time Kate waited to hear Ray coming through the trees behind them. Part of her *wanted* to hear him coming, because that would mean that she hadn't killed him. But what if she had? She'd hit him as hard as she could, and the sound had been terrible. What if she'd crushed his skull? She couldn't think about it.

They emerged at the fountain. There were a few skateboarders and other people still hanging around, but none of them said a word as the girls carried Mallory out of the park and toward the car.

CHAPTER 11

"We have to get her to a hospital," Annie said.

They were in the car. Cooper was driving and Annie was sitting beside her. Mallory was in the backseat, stretched across the laps of Kate, Sasha, and Becka. Sasha was rubbing her friend's hair and speaking softly to her.

"It's going to be okay," she said over and over, sounding like a mother comforting a sick child. "It's going to be okay."

Mallory still hadn't opened her eyes. She was breathing, so they knew she was alive, but none of them knew how injured she might be.

Cooper drove as quickly as she could without risking getting into an accident. When they reached the hospital she tore into the emergency room parking lot and pulled up to the doors. She and Annie got out and helped pull Mallory from the backseat while the others scrambled out after her. Three of them carried the unconscious girl while Annie and Kate ran ahead to the reception desk.

"We need help," Annie said to the receptionist. "Our friend is hurt."

The receptionist eyed Mallory as the other three carried her up to the desk. The receptionist motioned to someone behind her and moments later two men wheeled out a gurney while a woman and a man wearing blue hospital scrubs followed behind. The orderlies took Mallory from the girls and lay her on the gurney. The woman began checking her while the man turned to the girls.

"I'm Dr. Vargas and this is Dr. Madden," he said, nodding toward his colleague. "What happened?"

"She fell off some rocks we were hanging around on," answered Sasha.

A look of suspicion passed briefly over the man's face. Then he was all business again. "First things first," he said, turning to help Dr. Madden examine Mallory.

"How long has she been unconscious?" Dr. Madden asked.

"About twenty minutes," Sasha told her.

The two doctors opened Mallory's eyes and shined a light in them. "What's her name?" asked the man.

"Mal—" Kate began, but Sasha interrupted her.

"Denise," Sasha said.

Dr. Vargas nodded, regarding Sasha closely for a moment. "Denise," he said to Mallory. "Can you hear me?"

Mallory didn't respond.

"Let's get her into a room," said Dr. Madden.

The orderlies wheeled Mallory away, with the woman doctor following them. Dr. Vargas turned to the girls. "Tell me exactly what happened," he said.

"She was climbing around on some rocks and totally wiped out," Sasha said, sounding frustrated. "What else is there to know?"

The doctor looked at Sasha as if he wanted to ask more questions. Instead he nodded. "Okay," he said. "You stay here and fill out the paperwork they're going to need. I'll see what I can find out about your friend."

"Sister," Sasha said. "She's my sister."

"Your sister," the man said. "Okay. Well, stay here. I'll be back as soon as I know something."

The doctor left the girls in the waiting area and followed after the other doctor and Mallory.

"Why did you tell him she's your sister?" Kate asked Sasha when he was gone.

"And why did you say her name was Denise?" Annie added.

Sasha sighed. "You guys don't get it," she said. "And I don't expect you to. Mallory is a runaway. Do you know what that means to people? She might as well be a piece of trash on the street. I didn't want them to treat her like that."

"I don't think they would treat her any differently," Becka said.

Sasha shot her a look. "They would," she said. "I know."

She turned and walked over to the receptionist. "What do I need to fill out?" she asked.

The woman handed her a clipboard holding a stack of forms. "This, for starters," she said. "We'll need to know what insurance she has, any health problems, that kind of thing. And we'll need contact information. Are you family?"

"Her sister," replied Sasha.

"Then we'll need to get your parents down here," the receptionist told her.

Sasha nodded. She took the clipboard and walked over to an empty chair. The other girls followed her and sat around her, watching as she filled in the first form.

"Are you just making everything up?" Cooper asked.

Sasha shrugged. "I don't have a choice," she said. "I don't know anything about her health or anything like that."

"What about this whole parent thing?" Annie asked her. "You can't just make that up. Someone is going to have to come down here."

"I know," answered Sasha. "One thing at a time, though."

They left her alone to fill out the forms. After a minute Kate got up and walked down the hall to the water fountain. Annie followed her. The two of them stood at the fountain and talked.

"This isn't good," Annie said. "We're going to have to tell someone who can help."

"I know," Kate responded. "But how? Sasha is totally paranoid about police and authority figures and all of that."

"What do you think she meant when she said she knows how hospitals treat runaways?" Annie asked.

"I'm not sure," said Kate, leaning down to take her third drink in an attempt to look like they were actually getting water and not holding a mini-conference. "Something else strange happened earlier. When Ray was threatening us, he said something about having once done something bad to Sasha. Maybe that has something to do with it."

"Maybe," Annie said thoughtfully. "But we're going to have to do something. For one thing, Ray is still out there."

Kate blanched. For a second she thought she might faint. Annie, seeing her face, asked, "Are you okay?"

Kate nodded. "I had to hit him," she said, her voice faint. "With a stone." She paused, unable to continue. The sound of the stone hitting Ray's head had come back to her with sickening clarity, and she felt her stomach rising. She managed not to throw up, but just barely.

"Did you—" began Annie, then stopped. She looked at her friend, and the unspoken question was in her eyes.

"I don't know," Kate said, knowing that Annie was asking if Ray was dead. "I hit him really hard, and he wasn't moving. He might be."

Annie bit her lip. "We really have to call some-one," she said.

Kate nodded. She knew Annie was right. "But who?" she asked. "We can't call my parents. They would totally freak."

"Cooper's dad is a lawyer," said Annie. "Maybe we should call him."

"He's still out of town," Kate reminded her. "What about your aunt?"

"I'd rather not," said Annie. "I'd hate Grayson to think that I was dragging his daughter into the middle of a gang war or something. Let's give him at least a month of living with me before I start calling with emergencies."

The two of them thought for a minute, coming up with nothing. Then Kate remembered something. "What about Detective Stern?" she suggested.

Detective Mick Stern had been assigned to the case involving the death of Elizabeth Sanger, a girl whose ghost had come to Cooper for help almost a year earlier. At first he had been skeptical about what the girls were telling him, but he'd come to believe them after Cooper had led him to the body and provided other clues to solving the mystery.

Annie and Kate looked at one another, both thinking about Detective Stern and whether or not calling him was a good idea. Neither said anything.

"What's going on?" Cooper asked, walking up to them. "We thought you guys might have gotten lost or something."

"We're talking about whether or not we should call Detective Stern and tell him about what happened," Kate said.

Cooper was taken aback. "Wow," she said. "Do you think that's a good idea?"

"We have to tell someone," Annie said. "I know Sasha is worried about getting anyone else involved, but we can't just pretend Mallory is her sister. What if Ray comes looking for her again?"

"Or what if I killed him?" Kate added, finally able to voice the one thought she'd been trying to avoid thinking about.

Cooper nodded. "You're right," she said. "We do need help. And if we have to talk to the cops, I'd definitely prefer it to be Detective Stern."

"Do we tell Sasha?" Annie asked, glancing down the hallway to where their friend still sat, her pen moving rapidly across yet another form.

"No," Cooper said. "She's got enough to worry about. I'll see if I can get Stern to meet us at the park. You guys go keep Becka and Sasha company while I make a call."

Annie and Kate returned to the waiting area while Cooper went in search of a pay phone.

"Hey," Becka said as they sat down. "Good news. Sort of. The doctor came back and said that Mallory— I mean Denise—is awake. She's still really out of it, and they've given her a lot of painkillers. I guess she has some internal injuries they need to look at more closely, and she probably has a concussion."

"But she's not going to die," Sasha said, summing up Becka's news in one succinct point.

"Right," said Becka.

"So she's okay?" Kate said anxiously.

"No, she's not okay," Sasha replied. "That jerk did a real number on her. But she's going to live." She looked at Kate. "I can't say I hope the same thing for him."

Kate looked down. She knew Sasha would be furious if she knew what Cooper was doing at that very moment. But she also knew that it was the right thing to do. Luckily, before anyone could say anything else, Cooper returned. Annie repeated the good news about Mallory to her.

"That's great," Cooper said. "Look, I have to run home for a minute. And Kate, you said you needed to get something at your house too, right?"

"Right," Kate said, playing along.

"Why don't we go take care of that and grab some food for everyone?" suggested Cooper.

"Good idea," Annie said brightly.

Sasha had returned to filling out forms. "Social Security number?" she said with irritation. "How should I know that?"

"Okay then," Cooper said. "We'll be back in a little bit. Can you guys handle things here?" she added, looking at Annie.

"We'll be fine," answered Annie. "Go."

Cooper and Kate left and got back in the car.

"Did you get ahold of Detective Stern?" Kate

asked as soon as the doors were shut.

"Yeah," Cooper told her. "He's going to meet us at the park."

They drove back to the park. By now it was dark, and they were relieved to see that the detective was standing at the entrance to the park, waiting for them beneath a streetlight.

"Well," he said after they had parked and gotten out of the car. "We meet again." He looked at Cooper and grinned. "Any ghosts taken a bullet for you lately?" he asked.

"No," Cooper said. "But there's always a chance it will happen tonight."

"So, fill me in," the detective said. "You were a little mysterious on the phone. Your friend was attacked by some guy in here?"

"Back in the deserted pump house," said Cooper. "I'll show you."

Detective Stern followed as Cooper and Kate walked through the park, telling him bits and pieces of the story as they went. By the time they neared the clearing where the pump house was, he knew pretty much everything. At least everything the girls thought he needed to know.

"We left him right in there," Kate said, pointing into the pump house. "On the floor."

"Stay here," the detective told them.

"No problem," said Kate. She had no intention of going back inside the building. If Ray *was* dead, she knew she couldn't stand to see his body.

Already she was having flashbacks to the moment when the rock had collided with his head.

Detective Stern went inside. He emerged a moment later. "There's nobody here," he said. "Some blood, but no dead guy."

Kate breathed a sigh of relief, at least until Cooper said, "He might have gone back downstairs."

The detective turned around and went back inside. This time he was gone for a much longer time. When he finally came back out he said, "Nothing." He started to come down the steps when his flashlight picked up something on the steps leading to the entrance. He bent down and touched his fingers to the marble.

"Blood," he said, lifting his hand to his nose. He shined the flashlight farther down the steps. There was more blood. A trail of it led away from the old pump house and into the woods.

"Looks like you just hurt him," the detective said, returning to stand beside Kate.

Kate breathed a deep sigh of relief. Then a horrible thought occurred to her. "That means he's still out there," she said.

Detective Stern nodded. "Your friend is safe enough in the hospital." He hesitated before continuing, "You know, technically I should report her as a located missing person."

Cooper looked at Kate, then back at Detective Stern. "Could you hold off on that for a while?" she asked him. "Sasha is totally freaked out about cops," she said. "I think she has the right idea about asking her mother to help for now. If we can get Mallory somewhere safe, then we can work on the whole contacting-the-family thing. Okay?"

The detective let out a long sigh. "Why is it that whenever I talk to you I feel like I'm seven years old again and my brother is trying to talk me into lifting gum from Mr. Finnigan's drugstore?" he asked.

"Just a couple of days," Cooper said. "That's all I'm asking for."

"Fine," said the detective after a long wait. "I know I'll probably regret this, but okay."

"Thanks," said Cooper. "I knew we could trust you."

"Coming from you, that's a major compliment," said Detective Stern. "Now, before I let you off the hook totally, what can you tell me about this guy? We need to locate him and make an arrest, once we get an official statement."

"Tell you what," Cooper said. "We'll do a sketch of him tonight and I'll bring it by the station tomorrow."

Detective Stern chuckled. "You girls are something else," he said. "Are you sure you don't want to come work for me when you're old enough?"

"Sorry," Cooper replied. "What would Charlie do without us?"

"Charlie?" the detective said.

Kate and Cooper laughed. "You need to get to the movies more often," Cooper told him.

They walked back to their cars, where they said good-bye. Kate and Cooper drove back toward the hospital in reflective silence. When they were about halfway there Kate said, "I'm really glad I didn't kill him."

"Me, too," Cooper said. "I guess."

"What do you mean you guess?" Kate said sharply. "Do you want me to be a murderer?"

"No," Cooper said, not sounding at all sure of that. "But I *would* like to see Ray get what he deserves."

"Yeah, well, *that* I agree with," Kate said as they pulled into the parking lot of a fast-food place so that they could get the dinner they'd promised the others. "But how? We can't just hunt him down like a bunch of vigilantes."

"No," Cooper said. "We can't. At least not unless we want to get in trouble. But maybe there is something we can do."

"What's that?" asked Kate, getting out and shutting the door.

Cooper looked at her friend over the top of the car. "Maybe we can zap him a little."

"Zap him?" Kate repeated, not understanding.

"As in 'so mote it be'?" Cooper said.

"Oh," Kate said, getting it. "You mean do a spell?"

Cooper nodded. "It's a thought," she said.

Kate smiled. "Detective Stern was right," she said. "You *are* bad."

"You love it," Cooper said as she came around the side of the car and took Kate by the arm. "Think it over. Right now we need to pick up some dinner. You must be starving after the beating you gave that creep."

"Now that you mention it," Kate said as they went into the restaurant, "I *could* use a cheese-burger."

The lower lip Cooper said as she came around the side of the car and took Kate by the arm. "Rank drove right now. We need to pick up some dinner. You must be starving after the beating your dad that drew.

Now after you mention it, Kate said as they went into the restaurant. I could go for a big burger.

CHAPTER 12

"We're meeting at Annie's house after school," Cooper told Kate when she saw her at school the next morning.

Kate yawned. She was exhausted. Cooper had dropped her off after the two had eaten and picked up food for the others. She was totally shaken from her encounter with Ray, plus there was no way her parents would allow her to be out much later, unlike Cooper's mom or Annie's aunt. Cooper had returned to the hospital and discovered Thea with Annie, Sasha, and Becka. Annie and Becka had convinced Sasha to call her mother and have her come down. Thea had taken control of the situation with the hospital and had told them that Denise, as they were still calling Mallory, was in her charge. Thea was a familiar presence at the hospital because of her work with children's services, so nobody questioned her.

Cooper had then taken Thea aside and told her about having gone to Detective Stern, and asked her not to say anything to Sasha about it. Thea agreed, and so they had sat as a group until the two doctors who had first looked at Mallory came out to tell them that, for the moment, Mallory was okay. They still needed to do some more tests before they knew the extent of her injuries, but there was no point, they said, in everyone hanging around all night. Sasha had wanted to stay anyway, but Thea had convinced her that she needed to get some sleep. Finally they had all gone home.

"What exactly are we doing?" Kate asked as they got their books out of their lockers.

"I'm not sure yet," replied Cooper. "Think about it during the day."

They split up, Kate going to her English class and Cooper heading for Algebra. As the period wore on, Kate tried not to let her tired mind wander too much. But she couldn't help thinking about what kind of ritual they could do that night. What sort of magic did you work to try to stop someone from doing something bad? They'd never really talked about that in class. Then again, she, Cooper, and Annie had experienced a *lot* of things that they'd never talked about in class. Kate was sure that they would come up with something good.

Her challenge for the moment was simply to stay awake, and that wasn't easy. Besides, Mr. Tharpe's voice was very mellow and soothing. *It would be so nice*, she thought, *to simply close my eyes and drift off*.

The next thing she knew, she was standing on the steps of the fake temple, looking inside. It was nighttime, and a silver moon hung overhead. Fog swirled around the steps, and she was cold. She was also, she realized, alone.

Suddenly a black form rushed at her from the back of the temple. She heard an evil laugh, and saw the shape raise its arm, ready to bring the stone in its hand down on her head. "I got her," a voice said. "I got her, and you're next."

Kate woke up just as the horrific shadow reached her. She was still in her seat, and Mr. Tharpe was still talking. No one had seen her doze off. *It must have only been for a minute or so*, she thought dully as she sat up and shook herself awake.

She knew that the shadow in the temple had been Ray. But it wasn't the flesh-and-blood Ray; it was almost like all of the badness in him had taken shape. She had seen the part of him that was able to do the horrible things he did, and it had frightened her terribly. Now she knew more than ever that they had to do the ritual that night. Ray had to be stopped.

But how? That was the question they had to answer.

Before she could, though, the period ended and it was time for the next one. She went through the whole day in this way, slogging through her classes and counting the minutes until the day was over. She was anxious to regroup with the others, to see what had happened during the day and to do the ritual.

Finally the last bell sounded and she went to her locker to meet Cooper. "Was this the longest day, or what?" Cooper asked her as they put their books away and grabbed their coats.

"Tell me about it," Kate answered. "I was so distracted I didn't even yell at Sherrie once during lab this afternoon. I think that freaked her out more than if I *had* yelled at her, though, so maybe I'm on to something."

The two of them left and drove straight to Annie's house, where Annie's aunt let them in. "The girls are upstairs," she told them. "Go on up."

They found Becka and Annie seated on the floor, looking at Tarot cards.

"Hey," Annie said. "I was just showing Becka the new deck I got at Crones' Circle."

"I take it you didn't tell your aunt about our little adventure last night," Cooper remarked as she removed her coat and hung it on the back of Annie's desk chair.

"Not exactly," Annie said. "I told her a friend of ours from class had an accident and that we had gone to the hospital, but I didn't give her details."

"She didn't seem to notice all that much anyway," added Becka. "She and my dad were all wrapped up in figuring out how to rearrange the house."

"Rearrange the house?" Kate said. "Why?"

Annie and Becka looked at each other. "I can't believe we forgot to tell you," Annie said. "I must have forgotten once everything started to happen."

"What?" Cooper said, echoing Kate's earlier question.

"My dad and I are moving here," Becka told them.

Kate and Cooper could barely contain their enthusiasm. "That's great!" exclaimed Kate.

"Yeah," Becka said. "They told us the other day, right before we all went to the park to warn Mallory."

"When are you moving?" Cooper asked her.

"June," Becka answered. "Right after school ends."

"But isn't the wedding in April?" Cooper asked.

"Yes," said Annie. "But Aunt Sarah and Grayson say they can't do two such stressful things at the same time. So they'll get married in April and then Grayson and Becka will go back to San Francisco for a few weeks."

"We're going to pack up our stuff and send it up here before we actually come," Becka said. "That way Dad says when we move it will feel more like we're going on vacation."

"Makes sense to me," said Cooper. She went over and gave Becka a hug. "Welcome to the family."

"Thanks," Becka told her. "It already feels like home here, so I think it will be pretty easy."

"Now that we've told you our news," Annie said, "we should talk about the ritual. Do you guys have any ideas?"

"What about Sasha?" asked Kate. "Shouldn't we wait for her?"

"She'll be here in a little while," Annie said. "She called from the hospital right before you got here."

"How's Mallory?" Cooper asked.

"Pretty much the same," said Annie. "She's drugged up pretty heavily because of all the pain, so she mostly sleeps. Sasha said she recognized her, though, so that's good. And the doctors said that there's nothing majorly wrong with her. Just a lot of bruises that will take a while to heal."

"Has anyone talked about what to do next?" Kate said. "You know, about contacting her family or whatever?"

"I don't think Sasha can think about that right now," Annie said. "She's too tired and worried."

"It can wait," said Cooper. "Tonight we need to focus on doing this ritual."

"Well, I've been thinking about it," said Annie. "We all know that we aren't supposed to use magic to harm anyone."

"Right," Cooper said. "Like the Wiccan Rede says, 'And it harm none, do as you will.'"

"We can't do anything to try to *hurt* Ray," Annie continued.

"You mean we *shouldn't* do anything to hurt him," Kate suggested.

Annie gave her a look and Kate shrugged. "So I was thinking that maybe we should do a ritual that sort of bends the rules a little bit," Annie finished.

"Bends the rules?" Cooper said. "I like the sound of that, but what do you mean?"

"Well, the other part of the Rede is that whatever energy you send out comes back to you three times as strong, right?" explained Annie. "So what if we do a ritual designed to make the energy Ray has been putting out there come back to *him* three times as strong?"

The others thought about what she was saying for a minute. Then Cooper gave Annie an approving look. "You mean do something to hurry along his karmic spanking, so to speak," she said.

"Exactly," Annie replied. "We can do something asking the universe to use his own energy against him. We wouldn't be doing anything bad to him ourselves, but we'd be teaching him a lesson."

Cooper looked at Kate. "What do you think?" she asked.

Kate nodded. "I think it's a good idea," she said. "But we've never done anything like that. How would it work?"

"I've been thinking about that, too," Annie said. "I think we need to raise energy somehow, the way we usually do during rituals. Then we need to send it out into the universe, directing it at Ray." She looked at the others, who nodded in agreement. "Oh, and I think we should ask one of the crankier goddesses for some help," she added.

"Come again?" Kate asked.

"You know," said Annie, "one of the goddesses who likes to kick butt every now and then. I was thinking maybe Kali."

Kate looked hesitant. "I don't know," she said. "Don't you remember what happened when I asked Oggun to do me a favor like that?" She didn't want to go into the whole story, primarily because it had involved her trying to get revenge on Annie and Tyler for their little indiscretion, and she didn't want to bring that up again. But Annie had cut her hand quite badly as a result of Kate's asking the Santerian god for help. In fact, she still had the scar as a reminder.

Annie rubbed her finger, as if feeling the place where her stitches had been. "I know," she said. "But this is different. We're not asking for revenge, exactly. We're asking that the energy Ray put out be turned back toward him."

Kate thought about it for a minute. It was true, they weren't asking the Goddess to hurt Ray. They weren't even necessarily suggesting that something bad happen to him. They were just asking for the Law of Three to be enacted. That didn't seem so bad.

"Okay," said Kate. "I think it sounds good."

"Great," Annie said. "Then when Sasha gets here we can start."

"Should I really be involved in this?" asked Becka. She'd been silent during the whole conversation. Now she was looking at the three girls with a questioning expression. "I mean, I know I've learned some stuff about magic and Wicca from Annie—and from books and stuff—but it's not like I'm in the same league as you guys."

"You've helped me with rituals before," Annie told her.

"And Sasha isn't in the group, either," Cooper said. "I mean technically. There's no reason the two of you can't be part of the ritual, though. The more people we have raising energy, the better."

As Cooper finished speaking Sasha walked in. She looked exhausted, as if she hadn't slept at all.

"Do you feel as bad as you look?" Cooper asked her.

"Worse," said Sasha, sinking onto Annie's bed and reclining against the pillows. "I've been at the hospital all day, and I only slept for maybe half an hour last night."

"But Mallory is going to be okay, right?" asked Kate. "So you can relax a little bit."

Sasha groaned. "It's not just what happened to Mallory," she said. "This whole thing has brought up a lot of really awful memories. I just wish Ray was out of the picture permanently, if you know what I mean."

"I'm sorry I didn't hit him harder," Kate said.

"I didn't mean it that way," said Sasha, sitting up. "It's just that I thought that part of my life was behind me for good. Now it's right here in Beecher Falls."

"Well, we have a plan to maybe get it out of

Beecher Falls," Annie told her. She explained their idea for a ritual to Sasha.

"Sounds good to me," Sasha said when Annie was done explaining. "So, you want to ask Kali for help, huh?" she added.

"I thought she'd be good," said Annie.

"Can I ask who Kali is?" Becka said sheepishly. "I mean, I know she's a Hindu goddess, but why her?"

Cooper looked at Annie. "Professor Crandall, would you like to explain?" she said.

Annie made a face at Cooper. "Hinduism basically divides the deities into three groups," Annie told Becka. "There are the creators, the sustainers, and the destroyers. Kali is one of the destroyers, at least some of the time."

"That sounds really grim," remarked Becka.

"Not really," Annie told her. "It's all part of the natural cycle of birth, death, and rebirth. Kali is a destroyer because it's believed that when she gets angry she devours the demons of ignorance and anyone who follows them. She destroys things that need to be destroyed so that new things—good things—can be created."

"Kind of like a killing frost," Cooper said thoughtfully.

"Whatever," Annie said. "The point is, I thought she would be a good goddess to ask for help because what we're really trying to do is destroy the evil that Ray creates with his actions."

"Got it," Becka said. "So, what do we do?"

"Kali likes fire," said Annie. "She also likes drumming and chanting. I thought we could make a circle with some red candles and then raise energy by doing those things."

"We need a chant," Cooper said.

"That's *your* job," Annie told her. "While we set up the circle, you write."

"Why do I always get the hard stuff?" complained Cooper as the others got up to help Annie.

For the next fifteen minutes Annie, Sasha, Kate, and Becka set up the sacred circle. They cleared the floor in the middle of the room and arranged red candles in a circle. Annie put her small cauldron in the center of the circle to represent more fire. Then she produced a small drum from her closet.

"I picked it up at the store," she said. "You know, because of the workshop and all."

"How's that chant coming?" Kate asked Cooper, who had been busily writing.

"Not bad," Cooper said. "Almost done."

"Good," Annie said. "We'll start in a few minutes, then."

They lit the candles while Cooper wrote the last of the chant. Then she joined them inside the perimeter of the circle. Annie turned off the lights and the room glowed with a fiery light.

"I'll cast, if that's okay," Annie said. "I have an idea for something good."

She looked around at her friends, and they all nodded. She then picked up one of the candles and held it in front of her. Walking clockwise around the circle, she said, "One time 'round I cast the circle with the fire of protection. May this circle be a place of safety and refuge." She then walked around again, this time saying, "Two times 'round I cast the circle with the fire of justice. May this circle be a place of strength and fury." The third time around she said, "Three times 'round I cast the circle with the fire of renewal. May this circle be a place of cleansing and healing."

When she was done she returned the candle to its place in the perimeter and said, "The circle is cast. Let us make magic."

The girls sat down in the circle of fire. Annie turned to Kate. "Would you like to invoke Kali?" she asked.

Kate nodded and stood up. She stood in the center of the circle and held up her hands. "Kali," she called out. "The Destroyer. Mother of Death and Change." She thought about what Kali represented, and about what they wanted her help in doing. Then she continued speaking. "If you will, join us in our circle tonight. Lend to us your gifts of strength and anger. Help us create magic that will change what has been made wrong and destroy the hatred that has harmed our friend Mallory. Devour the evil that we seek to end."

When she was finished she sat down again. "How was that?" she asked, not sure if she'd done a good enough job.

"Perfect," Cooper said. "Very forceful."

Kate looked at Becka, who was watching everything with interest. "It's not an exact science," she remarked. "We kind of make up a lot of it as we go along."

"Okay," Annie said. "I think it's time we raised some energy. Cooper, do you want to teach us the chant?"

Cooper held up the paper she'd been writing on. "It's not perfect," she said, "but I think it will do. I'll sing it through once and then you guys can join in." She cleared her throat and then sang:

> In the belly of the cauldron,
> in this circle made of flame,
> call we up the burning power,
> conjure it in Kali's name.

> Strength and anger, rage and fury,
> fuel the flames and raise them higher,
> fill them with our mighty spirit,
> form a ring of cleansing fire.

> Crackling, sparking, never fading,
> fire pure and fire wild,
> go and do our magic bidding,
> go avenge the Mother's child.

She looked around. "Got it?" she asked.

Everyone nodded. Annie began playing a simple

beat on her drum. After a moment Cooper began the chant, followed soon after by the others. They sang the entire chant through three times, then Annie said, "Imagine our voices and the sound of the drum producing energy. Imagine it rising up inside the cauldron and forming a living flame, bright and powerful. Picture it bubbling in the cauldron, growing stronger and fiercer with our intentions."

They chanted some more. Some of them closed their eyes. Others clapped along with the rhythm. Their voices became stronger and louder, and Annie's drumming matched them.

Then, as if by some signal, they reached out and took one another's hands, forming a living circle. Annie stopped drumming but they all kept singing for a few more minutes.

"Now imagine the flame we've created leaving the circle," Annie instructed them. "Imagine Kali scooping it up in her cauldron and sweeping across the night sky to wherever Ray is. Imagine her finding him and pouring the fire over him. See it encircling him, trapping him inside of it. He isn't burned, but he can't move. The fire is our energy, our intention to keep Ray trapped."

She paused, letting this image fill their minds. Then she continued. "Imagine Ray fighting the fire," she instructed them. "Picture him trying to put it out with his anger and his rage. But no matter how hard he tries, his energy is turned against him. It makes the fire stronger. Three times as strong as his own emotions. It feeds off him, turning his hate into love and making the flames grow higher and brighter."

The five girls sat quietly in the silent room. Around them the candles seemed to burn more intensely, more brightly. The air was shimmering with the heat, and with something else. When they looked at one another, it was like looking through white fire. Their faces glowed, and their linked hands were hot to the touch.

"I think we did it," Annie said, smiling at everyone.

"It's amazing," Becka said, her voice filled with awe. "I could feel everything and see everything just the way you described it."

"Go, Kali," said Sasha, nodding her head appreciatively. "She was *here*, guys. I could tell."

"I think so, too," said Cooper. "Good work, everyone."

"Now what happens?" Becka asked.

"We wait," Annie said.

"And we hope Ray isn't wearing fire-retardant clothes," Cooper added.

CHAPTER 13

What are we doing here? Cooper wondered as she looked around the room. They were in the basement of a church, sitting on metal folding chairs and holding cups of coffee. Her mother was sitting beside her, anxiously picking pieces from the edge of her cup, while next to Mrs. Rivers, Mrs. McAllister kept up a steady stream of conversation.

"I've been coming here nearly every Friday night for six years," she told them.

Cooper scanned the walls of the basement, which were covered with colorful banners featuring Bible verses and inspirational sayings. A large picture of Jesus holding a lamb hung directly opposite her chair, and stacks of hymnals sat beside a battered old upright piano tucked away in the corner. The basement was carpeted with a rug whose once-golden color had faded to a dull yellowish brown, tarnished with the dirt of the thousands of pairs of shoes that had walked across it in the who-knew-how-many years since it had first been put there. The smell that permeated the place was a combination of dampness, old coffee, and perfume, the last scent courtesy of a small, nervous-looking woman who sat a few seats away from them, smiling at everyone and then ducking her head to avoid their return smiles.

She looked more closely at the basement she was in. Maybe it wasn't like being in a circle ringed with candles while someone drummed and the others chanted. But it was a sacred place of its own, a place where people came to hold their own kind of rituals with their own purposes. *Maybe I'm not such a stranger here after all,* she thought.

About a dozen people were now milling about the room, most of them women. One of them, a woman who could easily have been Cooper's grandmother, clapped her hands. "Okay," she called out, "let's circle up."

Cooper's ears perked up at the word *circle*. She watched as the people in the room claimed chairs and then began arranging them in a circle. She scooted her own chair over so that she was seated between her mother and a man who set his chair down beside her. He smiled and nodded at Cooper, and she nodded in return.

With the circle formed, the grandmotherlike woman who had called them together looked around. "I don't know everyone," she said. "That means some of you are new or guests, so introductions are in order. My name is Rhoda."

The woman beside Rhoda went next, introducing herself as Beth. They continued around the circle until coming to Cooper's mother. Cooper watched, waiting to see what she would say. Her mother was still fidgeting with her coffee cup.

"I'm Janet," she said finally, her voice coming out like air being forced through a very small hole. She cleared her throat and said again, "I'm Janet."

"I'm Cooper," Cooper said, following her mother.

The recitation of names continued on with Ralph, the man next to Cooper, and then around the circle until they returned once again to Rhoda. She looked around at everyone once more.

"Welcome," she said. "It's wonderful to see old friends as well as new ones. Now let me tell you a little about who we are. First of all, we are not a twelve-step program."

There was some scattered laughter from the group at Rhoda's announcement. She continued. "This is not AA or Al-Anon or any of those things," she said. "What this is is a group of people who have been affected by alcohol. Some of us *have* been through programs like AA. Some of us are *in* programs like AA. But that's not what we are. We're simply a group that meets to talk about our lives. Sometimes we help each other. Sometimes we just listen. We don't preach, we don't judge, and we don't try to get you to do or say anything you don't want to."

Cooper snuck a glance at her mother. Mrs. Rivers was looking at Rhoda. From time to time she looked at some of the other people as well, but only for brief moments before turning her attention back to the woman who was leading the circle.

Circle. There it was again, Cooper realized. They were all sitting in a circle. Perhaps their purpose in being there wasn't quite like the purpose behind a Wiccan circle, but there were definitely similarities.

"We work very informally," Rhoda was saying. "If you want to talk, you talk. Otherwise you listen. When someone is talking, we don't interrupt or comment. We listen. So, does anyone have anything to say?"

Cooper found herself becoming a little tense. It was always awkward for her, being in groups where people spoke when they were moved to. It made her feel like she was supposed to say something, if only to fill the silence that always threatened to overwhelm things. And now she found herself becoming even more tense because she was waiting to see if her mother would talk.

It had taken a lot of coaxing to get her mother to agree to come to the group Mrs. McAllister was a part of. At first she had insisted that she didn't need to talk about what was going on with her. She'd said she would be fine. But when Cooper had returned home on Thursday night after her ritual with her friends, she'd found her mother sitting at the kitchen table, staring at an unopened bottle of vodka. "I think now I'm ready to talk to Mary," she'd said to Cooper as her daughter had stood anxiously in the doorway, watching her.

The two women *had* talked, and the result was that they were all three sitting in the church basement, with Cooper alternately terrified that her mother wouldn't speak and then that she would. It had been Mrs. McAllister's idea that Cooper come. "After all," she'd said, "this is about you, too."

There was, of course, one member of the Rivers family not present. Cooper's mother had asked Cooper not to mention the meeting to her father. Cooper knew it was because her mother was embarrassed, although she'd been a little bit puzzled about how going to the meeting was any more embarrassing than having Mr. Rivers see her drunk. Still, she'd done as her mother asked. She hadn't, however, told her that she was scheduled to have dinner with her father later that same night, not wanting to do anything that might make her change her mind about attending the meeting.

"My name is Brandon," said a man across the circle from Cooper. She looked at him. He appeared to be not much older than she was. When everyone turned to look at him, he blushed slightly and looked at his feet.

"I'm a student," he said, "at the college. It's the first time I've been away from home and living on my own." He paused. No one spoke or interrupted him, giving him the time he needed to continue. "It's harder than I thought," he said finally. "You have all of this freedom. A lot of my friends like to party, and there's always stuff to drink, you know?"

Brandon stopped talking again. The look on his face suggested that he thought he might have said something stupid. Cooper watched him. She knew how he felt. He was telling a bunch of strangers something about himself that he wasn't very happy about. She had a difficult time talking to people she trusted about her life; she couldn't imagine doing what he was doing.

"I don't think I'm an alcoholic or anything," said Brandon. "I mean, my dad was one, so I know what that's about. But it's so easy to drink when there's pressure." He looked around. "I guess I'm just wondering how people find ways not to drink," he concluded.

Rhoda and some of the others nodded. Several people looked at Brandon, as if making sure he didn't have anything else to say. Then a woman a few chairs away from Mrs. McAllister spoke.

"I'm Joan," she said, "and I have a *very* clean house."

The others laughed. When they were quiet again Joan resumed speaking. "I *am* an alcoholic," she said. "I never needed an excuse to drink. But when I stopped, I needed to find other things to do instead of drinking. I tried eating, but when I had to buy new clothes every two months I figured that was probably just as bad as drinking. So I tried a lot of other things. Finally I settled on cleaning. I know, it's just another kind of addiction, but at least my bathroom is shiny."

Again people laughed. Joan gave a small smile. "It sounds funny," she said. She looked at Brandon. "But it isn't really funny when it's happening to you. You feel like if you don't find *something* else to do you're going to go right for that drink. So I clean. Sometimes I run, or bike, or bake cookies—something *fun*. Drinking seems like fun, but for a lot of us it's just a substitute for fun. Do something you enjoy."

Brandon nodded at her. Cooper wondered how it felt for him, hearing Joan's story. Did he relate to it? After all, his situation seemed different from hers. Was what she said helpful?

"I started drinking because everyone else was doing it," said a man next to Brandon. He reminded Cooper of her father. "I was in the army," he continued. "All my buddies drank, so I did, too. And it was *fun*," he added, looking at Joan and smiling so that she laughed.

"But it wasn't fun when I started passing out," the man continued, sighing. "That's when I needed to find a way to stop. But it was like my buddies didn't want me to. They kept inviting me out to bars with them, kept offering me beers. Saying no was one of the hardest things I've ever done. But then I realized that they wanted me to drink with them because *they* felt lonely and scared. They wanted to feel better about what they were doing by getting me to do it, too. That's when it got easy to say no." He laughed to himself. "Well, *easier*," he said.

For the next half hour various people told their stories. None of them directly offered Brandon any advice. None of them lectured him or tried to tell him what to do. They just shared their stories. Listening to them, Cooper realized that what they were doing was creating intention. Much as she and her friends raised energy by chanting, drumming, or singing, they were creating energy, energy that Brandon—or anyone—could use if he wanted to. They were putting the power of their stories into the circle so that they could become something else and create change.

Throughout the meeting, Cooper's mother listened carefully. Sometimes she nodded. Other times she sat staring into space, as if she had tuned out what was being said, or maybe was thinking about it more deeply. From time to time Cooper thought she sensed her mother was about to speak, but she never did. When the meeting ended, she hadn't said a word.

"That's it for tonight," Rhoda said when it was time to end. "Remember, what is said here stays here. Also remember that even when the group isn't together, you still have people you can talk to if you need to. Contact lists are on the table. Feel free to take a copy and use it."

She's opening the circle, thought Cooper, thinking

of the traditional Wiccan saying, "The circle is open, but unbroken." She'd always liked that way of ending a ritual. It made her remember that what was created in a circle had a life of its own, that it didn't end or fade away just because the physical circle wasn't there. Once again she was struck by the fact that these people were also working a kind of magic of their own, a kind of magic that could potentially transform lives.

Everyone stood up and began mingling, talking to one another and heading for more coffee. Mrs. McAllister turned to Mrs. Rivers. "Not so bad, was it?" she said.

Mrs. Rivers shook her head. "No," she said. "It wasn't so bad." She looked at Cooper. "Thanks," she said. "For talking to Mary and for coming tonight."

"Any time," Cooper told her mother. She knew that saying thank-you was hard for her mother, just like it was often hard for her. She hoped that her mother really had gotten something from the meeting.

"So, will you come with me next week?" Mrs. McAllister asked.

Cooper held her breath. She knew how her mother felt about self-help groups. She knew, too, that Mrs. Rivers didn't consider herself an alcoholic. Neither, really, did Cooper. But she was definitely going through something, and maybe coming back to the circle again would help her be able to talk about that.

After a long pause Mrs. Rivers nodded. "Yes," she said. "I'll come back."

Cooper gave a silent cheer upon hearing her mother's words. She wanted to hug Mrs. McAllister. She wanted to hug her mother. Instead, she stood up and stretched. "I have some plans with some friends," she said. "I've got to run."

"Fine," Mrs. McAllister teased, "leave us all alone on a Friday night." She looked at Mrs. Rivers. "Ungrateful child. She's probably running off to see a movie with my son."

Cooper pretended to be offended. "For your information," she said, "I am *not* running off to see your son. He and his band are playing tonight."

Mrs. McAllister shook her head. "That's okay," she said. "If your mother is up to it, I have plans of my own. I thought we'd have a girls' night out. Maybe dinner and a movie?"

Cooper saw a strange expression come over her mother's face. She knew her mother didn't have a lot of friends, and certainly she didn't go out with them on Friday nights. She'd been married to Cooper's father for so long that she hadn't had the opportunity to do something like that in many years.

"Come on, Janet," Mrs. McAllister coaxed. "There's a new movie at the Omni."

Mrs. Rivers smiled, looking, Cooper thought, like someone who had just been asked to sit at the popular table at lunch. "Okay," she said. "Why not?"

Cooper looked at Mrs. McAllister over her mother's head. *Thanks*, she mouthed silently. Then she said to her mother, "I should be back by ten. I'll see you then."

"Okay," said her mother. Then she looked at Cooper. "But don't wait up."

Cooper gave a surprised look, earning laughs from her mother and Mrs. McAllister. Then she waved good-bye and left. As she walked down the street, heading for the restaurant where she'd arranged to meet her father, she couldn't help but think about how the things she'd learned—and was still learning—in her study of witchcraft kept coming up over and over again in the larger world. Where once she'd thought of Wicca as this little secret that only a few people shared, now she saw it as something much larger. It had become a way of thinking for her, a way of looking at things and seeing their interconnectedness.

She realized, to her surprise, that for the first time in her life she felt as if she was part of a group. But not a group like a clique of popular kids or a member of an exclusive society that kept other people out. Now she felt like she belonged to a group made up of all kinds of people. Some of them she knew, some of them she had yet to meet, and some she might never know. But still they were all connected. It didn't matter if some of them met in Wiccan circles and some of them met in church basements. They were all linked together.

"We are the weavers," she sang as she walked, thinking of the words to a chant they had sung in class once, "we are the web. We are the spiders, we are the thread."

She'd always liked that chant, with its images of spiders weaving beautiful webs connecting things to one another. Now it made even more sense to her. She was a maker of connections: between herself and her friends, between her mother and Mrs. McAllister, between herself and the Goddess. Every friendship she made—like the one with Jane—and every relationship she had—like the one with T.J.—was another link in a big chain. Each was also another step on the journey she was taking.

Where will it take me next? she asked herself as she reached the restaurant and went inside.

CHAPTER 14

"I'm so glad you guys came," said Annie as she hugged Becka good-bye on Saturday morning.

"And *I'm* so glad we're going to be sisters," Becka said.

"We'll see if you feel the same way once you move in," Annie joked, and they both laughed.

Grayson Dunning and Aunt Sarah were outside, standing beside the rental car that Grayson had just finished loading with his and Becka's bags. They were kissing. Meg, watching them from the doorway, said, "Are they going to do that all the time when you guys move here?"

"Probably," Becka replied. "So get used to it."

They all went outside for their final farewells. Aunt Sarah gave Becka a hug while Grayson did the same with Meg and Annie. As Becka climbed into the front seat she said quietly to Annie, "Let me know how everything works out with Mallory."

Annie nodded. "I'll call you tonight," she said.

After the car drove away, Annie, her aunt, and

Meg went back inside. Aunt Sarah closed the door and stood in the entryway, looking around. "This place could use some paint," she said thoughtfully.

Annie looked at Meg. "Uh-oh," she said. "She's redecorating. You know what that means."

"I'm out of here," Meg said, heading for her room.

"Hey!" Aunt Sarah said, pretending to be hurt. "I only changed my mind three times about the living room color. Give me a break."

"Yeah," Meg called back. "But *we* were the ones who had to repaint it every time."

The phone rang, sparing Annie from having to get involved in the conversation. Secretly she was siding with Meg. Her aunt did have a habit of frequently changing her mind about things like paint colors, and Annie was in no hurry to wield a brush again. She went into the kitchen and picked up the ringing phone.

"Hi," said Juliet. "How's my little sister today?"

"Hey," Annie said, happy to hear from her. "Great. Becka and Grayson were here for a few days. They just left, and now Aunt Sarah is playing Martha Stewart. You saved me from having to help her pick out paint colors."

"I'm glad I could be of service," Juliet replied. "So, how was the visit?"

"Well, it looks like our house is going to have two new occupants," Annie told her. "Becka and Grayson are moving in. Hence the paint colors."

"I get it," Juliet said, laughing. "Aunt Sarah wants everything to be perfect."

"You got it," said Annie. It made her happy to hear Juliet call Sarah "aunt."

"So, what else has been going on?" Juliet asked her.

Annie thought about where to start. She hadn't talked to Juliet in a while, since before everything with Mallory had happened. Should she tell her about it? Juliet already felt like family to her, but the fact was, they didn't know a whole lot about one another yet. Annie hadn't even brought up the subject of her involvement in Wicca with her sister. Would Juliet be freaked out if Annie told her about what she and her friends had been going through during the past week?

"Not much," she answered, deciding that certain things could wait until she and Juliet had spent more time together. "I've been busy with school and stuff. How about you?"

"It's been crazy," said Juliet. "The theater is launching a new production next week, and we've been working insane hours getting the costumes done. Plus, I volunteer making costumes for one of the Mardi Gras floats, and that takes up a lot of time, too. Hey, speaking of Mardi Gras, are you going to come?"

"I really hope so," Annie said. "Aunt Sarah seemed okay with it, but she wanted to talk to you about it first."

"Wow," Juliet replied. "I can't believe I'm about to talk to my aunt. I'm so excited. Put her on when we're done. But first I wanted to ask if you got my card yet."

"I don't know," said Annie. "I haven't looked at the mail since Thursday. Let me check."

The mail for the Crandall household was always stacked in a pile on the kitchen counter. Usually, Annie checked it religiously, but she'd been so busy with Becka's visit and the situation with Mallory that she had completely forgotten to look at it and see if there was anything for her. Now she picked up the pile and sorted it. Mostly it was bills for her aunt, but toward the bottom of the pile she found an envelope addressed to her. It had Juliet's return address in New Orleans.

"Here it is," Annie told Juliet. "Should I open it?"

"I insist," Juliet said.

Annie slid her finger underneath the envelope's flap and opened it. She pulled out the card.

"It's pretty," she said, looking at the picture, which was of a New Orleans street.

"Look *inside*," said Juliet.

Annie opened the card and a photograph slid out. She caught it before it fluttered to the floor, and held it up to look at it.

"Is this you?" she asked excitedly.

"No, it's Madonna," Juliet said. "Of course it's me."

Annie looked at the picture. The girl in it was

beautiful. She had long blondish brown hair that hung down around her face in waves. Her brown eyes were wide and sparkling, and her nose turned up slightly at the end. She was wearing a costume, a dark red velvet dress with a crown of pink and red roses on her head.

"You look like me," Annie said breathlessly. "I mean me if I was beautiful," she added. She felt excited and sad at the same time. This was her sister.

"I thought you might like to see what I look like," said Juliet. "So, is there a family resemblance?"

"Most definitely," Annie answered. "You look a lot like Mom."

There was silence on the other end for a moment, then Juliet said, "I wish I could have seen her."

"So do I," said Annie. "But I can send you pictures."

"Thanks," Juliet said. "Send me ones of you and Meg and Aunt Sarah, too."

Aunt Sarah walked in at that moment and Annie motioned for her to come to the phone. "Speak of the devil," she said to Juliet. "Here's Aunt Sarah. I'm going to let you guys talk about you know what, okay?"

Juliet agreed and Annie handed the phone to her aunt. "It's your niece," she whispered, and smiled when Aunt Sarah's face lit up.

Annie stepped back and listened as her older sister and their aunt had their first conversation.

She wasn't sure what to expect. Part of her thought maybe there would be some kind of dramatic movie-of-the-week weepfest happening. But in reality the conversation sounded pretty much like a conversation she might have with one of her own friends. After some initial awkwardness, Aunt Sarah seemed to relax. She asked Juliet some questions about herself and then—from the half of the conversation Annie could hear—answered some of Juliet's.

Finally, after what seemed like an eternity, Aunt Sarah said, "Annie tells me you'd like her to come visit for Mardi Gras."

Annie felt herself tense up a little. She really wanted to visit Juliet, and soon. Plus, Mardi Gras would be a lot of fun. She hoped her aunt would say she could go.

"Mmm-hmm," said Aunt Sarah in response to something Juliet was saying. "Okay. Right."

Annie grew more and more anxious as the conversation went on. She hated that she was only getting one side of things. What was Juliet telling their aunt? Aunt Sarah asked some more questions, then looked at Annie. "Well," she said, "that all sounds really interesting."

Interesting, Annie thought. *What a horrible word. It could mean anything.* After all, people frequently said things were interesting when they really meant they sounded horrible. It was one of those vague words that people used when they didn't want to say what they really meant. Did her aunt mean that the idea was interesting but there was no way it was going to happen? Or did she mean that it really did sound interesting and that Annie could go? Suddenly, Annie thought she would go crazy if she didn't find out immediately.

"Well?" she said loudly, surprising herself with how anxious she sounded.

Aunt Sarah grinned. "Yes," she said. "You can go."

Annie surprised herself again by letting out a little squeal of joy. *Oh, Goddess*, she thought, embarrassed. *I sound like one of those girls at an N'SYNC concert.* But she didn't care. She was going to get to meet her sister, and in New Orleans during Mardi Gras. She couldn't believe it.

Aunt Sarah hung up the phone. "She said she'll call you back later," she told Annie. "She was shrieking more than you were, and I thought putting the two of you together would probably make the phone line short out."

Annie hugged her aunt. "Thank you, thank you, thank you," she said. "I can't tell you how cool this is."

"I think you just did," Aunt Sarah said, rubbing Annie's back.

Annie let go of her. "I wish you and Meg could come with me," she said.

Her aunt smiled. "I think the first time it should just be you two," she said. "Besides, I think we'll have Juliet come to the wedding in April. That would be a great time for her to meet everyone."

Annie beamed. "That's perfect!" she said. She couldn't believe how everything was falling into place. "Oh," she said, thinking of something, "I should make an album to take to Juliet. You know, pictures of Mom and Dad and us. See, she sent me one."

She handed the photo of Juliet to Aunt Sarah. Her aunt stared at it for a long time, then handed it back to Annie. "You should show Meg," she suggested.

"Good idea," answered Annie. "And then I have to go meet the girls." She kissed her aunt on the cheek. "Thank you again," she said.

She went to Meg's room. Her little sister was sitting at her desk, writing something in a notebook. Annie watched her from the doorway for a moment. Meg looked a lot like she had at that age, and Annie found herself thinking about what it would have been like for the three of them—her, Meg, and Juliet—to grow up together. They would never know, but at least they would get the chance to know one another now.

"Hey," Annie said. "Am I interrupting anything?"

Meg turned around. "I'm just writing a story," she said. "For Mr. Dunning," she added. "He liked the one I showed him while they were here, so I thought I'd write him another one."

"Now we'll have two authors in the family,"

Annie said. She stepped into the room. "Speaking of family," she said, "I have something to show you."

She handed Meg the photograph of Juliet. Meg took it and looked at it for a moment. "Is that her?" she asked.

Annie nodded. "She's pretty, isn't she?"

Meg shrugged. "Not as pretty as you," she said.

Annie watched Meg looking at the picture. Telling her sister about Juliet—and about why they'd never known about her—had been difficult. Meg was a very smart girl, but at ten there were things that were still difficult for her to understand. Annie knew that she didn't entirely comprehend why their parents had given Juliet up for adoption. She suspected that Meg was a little angry about it but didn't know why, and she'd been careful not to talk about the situation too much. She figured when Meg was ready to discuss it she would.

Meg handed the picture back to Annie. "Is she nice?" she asked. Meg still hadn't spoken to Juliet on the phone, nor had she asked to.

Annie nodded. "She's really nice," she said. "I think you're going to like her."

Meg didn't say anything in response. Annie wondered what she was thinking. There were so many changes going on in their lives at the moment, what with Aunt Sarah's marriage to Grayson and now the discovery of Juliet. Annie knew it was a lot for anyone to take in, much less a ten-year-old girl. After all, Meg had only ever lived with Aunt Sarah and Annie. She hadn't really known their parents. Now she had not only a new father figure, but another sister. *Two* new sisters, counting Becka.

"You know what?" Annie said. "We should do something tonight, just you and me."

"Really?" Meg said, sounding a little suspicious.

"Yeah," said Annie. "Anything you want—a movie, dinner, whatever."

"Anything?" repeated Meg.

"Anything," said Annie.

Meg grinned. "I want you to teach me some magic," she said.

Annie looked at her, taken aback. "What do you mean?" she asked.

"Come on," said Meg. "I'm not stupid. I know you and Kate and Cooper are doing magic up there. I want you to show me what you do."

Annie looked at her little sister. She knew that Meg had seen little bits and pieces of her Wiccan life, but she didn't know how much she knew or how much she understood. Was it time to tell her more about it? Was she old enough to understand that it wasn't just a game? Maybe it was.

"Okay," said Annie. "That's what we'll do. Tonight I'll show you what real magic is."

Meg nodded. "And pizza," she said. "I want pizza."

Annie laughed. "You drive a hard bargain," she

said. "But okay. Pizza and magic it is. Now I've got to go."

"And I have to write a story," said Meg.

Annie left the room and went to her own room. She set the photo of Juliet on her bedside table and grabbed her coat. Then she went downstairs to leave. She found her aunt standing in the entryway again, looking at the walls.

"Maybe blue," she said to Annie. "Or what about a nice brown? Brown is classic. Something earthy?"

"Got to run," Annie said lightly, opening the door and waving to her aunt.

"Some help you are," Aunt Sarah said, making a face.

Annie shut the door behind her and walked to the bus stop. She had agreed to meet the other girls at the hospital to visit Mallory. Sasha had called on Friday night to say that Mallory was finally coming out of her drugged state and could talk a little. She didn't remember anything about being attacked, and she was still in a lot of pain. But she didn't seem to have anything wrong with her that couldn't be fixed in time, and everyone was breathing more easily now that she was awake and speaking.

The bus ride was uneventful except for the fact that Annie ended up sitting next to a woman who insisted on telling her in unwelcome detail about her fifteen-year-old pug dog's digestive problems. Annie was relieved when they came to the hospital stop and she could escape, although the woman seemed to take her getting off the bus as some kind of personal attack and said, "Well, really," when Annie stood up to leave.

As it happened, Sasha, Kate, and Cooper were just arriving at the hospital as well. Annie saw them getting out of Cooper's car, and she waited for them at the entrance.

"We called to see if you wanted a ride, but you'd just left," Cooper said as they walked up. "Oh, and your aunt says she's decided on yellow, whatever that means."

Annie rolled her eyes. "She'll change her mind," she said.

They went inside and took the elevator to the fourth floor. As they passed the nurses' station the woman on duty looked up. "Oh, hello," she said when she saw Sasha.

The girls stopped. The nurses all recognized Sasha, and she had gotten to know most of them by name. "Hi, Dolores," Sasha said. "How's Denise doing?" They were still using the phony name that Sasha had come up with, more out of habit now than out of any real need.

"She's fine," the nurse replied. "Her brother is here."

"Brother?" Sasha said, confused. "What brother?"

It was the nurse's turn to look confused. "You don't know about her brother?" she said.

Sasha shook her head. She knew that Mallory

had a brother, of course, but there was no way he could be there. No one had even contacted him.

"He seems very nice," the nurse said. "Although he had a nasty bruise on his forehead, poor guy. He said he had a motorcycle accident a few days ago. That's why he hadn't come to see her yet, I guess."

Sasha looked at the others in horror. "Ray," she said.

"That's right," said the nurse. "I think that's what he said his name was."

"When did he get here?" Cooper asked.

"About ten minutes ago," said the nurse. "He's in there with her now."

"Call security," Cooper said as Sasha started racing for Mallory's room and the startled nurse looked after her. "Call them *now!*"

CHAPTER 15

"Get away from her!"

Sasha dashed at Ray, who was bent over Mallory. He took one look at the girls piling into the room and a nasty snarl crossed his face.

"Back off!" Cooper screamed at him.

Ray lunged past her and bolted from the room, shoving Annie and Kate in the process and knocking them down. As two security guards saw him and began running toward the room, Ray darted in the other direction. Cooper emerged from the room just in time to see him disappear around the corner.

"Is everyone okay?" the first guard to arrive asked.

Cooper glanced at Mallory and at Sasha. "Yeah," she said to the guard. "We're okay."

The guard nodded and left, chasing after Ray. Cooper went to Mallory's bedside. The girl was trying to sit up.

"I was asleep," she said, her voice raspy. "Someone shook me awake, and when I opened my eyes it was Ray." She paused, trying to swallow. "He told me he was going to kill me," she said. "Then he laughed."

Cooper grabbed Mallory's hand. "It's okay," she said gently. "He's gone."

"He'll be back," said Mallory, closing her eyes and leaning back against the pillows. "As long as he's alive, he'll come back. He won't give up until I'm dead."

Cooper looked at Sasha, who was now standing beside the bed.

"You okay?" Cooper asked her.

"I think so," Sasha said. She looked at Mallory. "She's right," she said. "He won't give up."

Annie and Kate had come to stand beside them. "So much for our ritual," said Kate glumly.

Several nurses ran into the room, looking anxiously at the girls.

"What happened here?" asked one of them, who was clearly in charge.

"Someone tried to kill her," Sasha told the nurse.

"He said he was her brother," said the nurse who had first spoken to them when they'd arrived. "He seemed so nice."

"It's okay," Cooper told the obviously distraught woman. "You didn't know."

"You four need to clear out of here for a while," said the head nurse to the girls. "We need to make sure the patient is okay."

Cooper bristled at the woman's treatment of

them, but she didn't say anything. She knew the nurse was just doing her job. And anyway, Mallory's well-being was more important than her pride. She nodded at the others and they filed into the hallway. As they were standing there the security guards who had come to their assistance appeared.

"Did you get him?" asked Sasha.

One of the guards shook his head. "He took the stairs," he said. "We lost him somewhere."

"Great," Cooper said, throwing her hands up. "Nice job."

The guards gave her a look. "I'm sorry," said the one who seemed to do all the talking. "There are a lot of hallways in this place, and a lot of doors. We aren't usually chasing would-be killers around here."

Cooper sighed. "We need to call Detective Stern," she said to her friends. Before they could reply she stormed off, giving the security guards a final disgusted look.

"Thanks for trying," said Kate to the guards, who were looking at each other sheepishly.

"What do we do now?" Sasha asked Kate and Annie.

"We can't really do anything about Ray," Annie said. "So we have to think about Mallory and what we can do for her."

"She needs to be somewhere safe," Kate said.

"Clearly that's not anywhere with us," said Sasha miserably.

"You said she had a brother," Annie said. "A real brother. Do you know where he is?"

Sasha sighed. "Not really," she said. "I mean, Mallory is from Maine. I guess he could live there. Their parents are dead, I know that. Mallory lived with her grandmother, but I don't know her name."

"Do you remember the name of the town?" Annie asked her.

Sasha thought. "It was a funny name," she said. "I remember thinking it sounded like something you would call a dog."

"Like Fido?" suggested Kate.

Sasha shook her head.

"Spot?" suggested Annie. "Rex?"

"King?" Kate said. "Digger? Fluffy? Humphrey?"

"Humphrey?" said Annie and Sasha together, looking at her.

"We had a dog named Humphrey once," said Kate.

"None of those are right," Sasha said.

They stood for a while, thinking and throwing out more names.

"Barkley?" Annie tried.

"Spike?" said Kate.

Sasha kept shaking her head. Then Annie said, "Rover?"

"That's it!" Sasha exclaimed.

"They live in Rover, Maine?" Kate said dubiously.

"No," Sasha said. "It sounded like Rover. That's why I thought of a dog name." She thought for a moment. "Dover. That was it. Dover, Maine."

"Let's go call information," Annie said. "And let's hope there's a Derek Lowell in Dover, Maine."

The three of them turned to go to the pay phones and almost smacked into Cooper.

"Now what?" she asked.

"We're going to try to call Mallory's brother," Kate explained.

"Did you get Detective Stern?" asked Annie.

Cooper nodded. "He's sending some guys over here to search the hospital," she said. "That's about all he can do."

The door to Mallory's room opened and the nurses came out. The head nurse walked over to the girls. "Your friend is fine," she said. "A little shaken up, as you can imagine, but fine."

"Thanks," Sasha told her. "Can I see her?"

The nurse nodded. "I think she'd like the company. Oh, and I'll get security to send someone up to guard the door, in case her 'brother' decides to make another appearance."

"I hope whoever it is does a better job than the other two," remarked Cooper under her breath, but Sasha said, "Thanks."

"You wait here with Mallory," Annie told Sasha. "We'll go see what we can find out about Derek Lowell."

Sasha nodded. "I'll stay, too," Cooper said. "Just in case."

Annie and Kate left the two of them there and headed for the phones. When they reached them, Annie plunked some change into the coin slot and dialed information. She gave the operator Derek's name. As she waited for the computer to search for the number, she looked at Kate. "I hope this works," she said.

"Here's the number," the operator told her. He read it to Annie and she recited it to Kate, who scribbled it on the back of a pamphlet on colonoscopies she found lying near the phones.

Annie hung up and Kate handed her the number. "Here you go," she said. "You call."

"Why me?" Annie asked. "I got the number."

"Because you sound the most stable," Kate said, and Annie rolled her eyes.

"Fine," she said. She put more money into the phone and dialed. As the phone rang and she waited for someone to answer, she suddenly became nervous. They didn't know anything about Derek Lowell except that he was Mallory's brother. He might not care where she was or what had happened to her. After all, she'd run away for some reason. Maybe he was it. Perhaps they were making a huge mistake. Annie started to hang up so that they could think it over.

"Hello?" said a woman's voice.

"Um, hi," Annie said, at a loss for words. "Is

Derek Lowell there?"

"Just a minute," the woman said. Then Annie heard her say, "Honey? It's for you. I don't know. A girl. Maybe one of your students."

A man's voice came on the line. "Hello?"

He sounds nice, thought Annie, trying to reassure herself.

"Mr. Lowell?" said Annie. "You don't know me. My name is Annie Crandall."

"If this is about the boating class, I'm afraid it's all filled up for the next session," said Derek.

"No," Annie said. "It's not about any lessons. It's about your sister. Mallory."

There was silence on the other end. Then Mr. Lowell said, his voice flat and hard, "Is this some kind of joke? Because if it is, it isn't funny."

"It's not a joke," Annie told him. She wasn't sure where to start. "Mallory is in the hospital," she began.

"Oh, my God," Derek said, sounding frightened. "Is she—" He left the question unfinished, but Annie knew what he was asking.

"She's okay," she said. "She just had a little accident."

She then told Derek the story, or at least the important parts. He had a lot of questions—questions she couldn't answer. "I wish I knew what she's been doing and where she's been," she told him, "but I don't."

"I'm coming out there," Mr. Lowell said. "I'm coming to bring her home."

Annie told him where they were. She also gave him her phone number at home so he could call if he needed any more information. He said he would call as soon as he'd confirmed a flight, and then Annie hung up.

"Well?" Kate said.

"He seems nice," said Annie. "I guess Mallory ran away more than two years ago. They had no idea where she was. For a while he was offering a reward for information about her, but no one ever called. At first he thought I was trying to get money out of him."

"So, he's coming?" Kate said.

Annie nodded. "As soon as he can get here," she said.

"Do you think we should tell Mallory?" asked Kate as they walked back toward her room.

"No," Annie said. "It might make her more upset. We still don't know exactly why she ran away, and she might not like it that we called Derek."

They reached the room, where a security guard was now standing by the door. He looked them over as they approached and then nodded at them to go in. When they entered they found Cooper and Sasha talking to a police officer.

"You have the sketch, right?" Cooper was asking the officer.

He nodded. "We're searching the parks and the usual places," he said. "I doubt this guy is stupid enough to go to any of them now, but you never know." He shut the notebook he was writing in.

The girls went to stand beside Mallory, who had her eyes open.

"You guys are like my personal bodyguards," she said. "Thanks."

"Ray really doesn't seem to like you all that much," said Cooper.

Mallory closed her eyes and opened them again. "He used to," she said. "Or at least he pretended to," she added, looking at Sasha. Sasha was looking at the floor, her face completely neutral.

"What exactly is it that you know that he doesn't want you to tell anyone?" Kate asked.

Mallory let out a long sigh. "There's a list," she said. "Take your pick. Robbery. Dealing. Assault." She blinked as tears started to flow from her eyes. "Murder," she said softly.

"Ray is your basic all-around no-conscience bad guy," said Sasha.

Mallory turned and looked at Sasha. "I'm sorry I didn't believe you," she said, her voice sad. "I didn't want to think he could do something like—what he did to you. I should have listened."

Sasha took her friend's hand. "It's okay," she said. "Forget about it." She looked at Annie. "Did you make that call you needed to make?" she asked, obviously changing the subject.

"Yeah," Annie said. "Everything is fine. We're all set."

Sasha nodded. Mallory had closed her eyes again, and seemed to have fallen asleep. Sasha started to let go of her hand, and Mallory opened her eyes. "Don't go," she said. "Stay with me, okay?"

Sasha smiled. "Sure," she said. She sat down in the chair beside the bed and rested Mallory's hand on her knee, their fingers still entwined. Mallory closed her eyes and settled into the pillows. A few moments later she was breathing quietly.

"Will you be okay alone?" Kate asked Sasha.

Sasha nodded. "I'll be fine," she said. "Just make sure the rent-a-cop outside is awake when you leave, okay? I don't think I could take Ray by myself."

The others waved good-bye to her, then they left, shutting the door behind them.

"Hey," Cooper said to the burly security guard who was leaning against the wall. "You keep an eye on that door. If anything happens to those two, I'm coming back and kicking your butt."

The guard stared after them as they walked away, an expression of confusion and surprise on his face.

"One of these days you're going to say that to

the wrong person," Annie told Cooper as they headed for the elevators.

"Maybe," Cooper said. "But by then I'll have learned how to knock a guy out cold with one punch."

CHAPTER 16

Kate took a deep breath before pushing open the door to the science lab. *I will not kill Sherrie*, she repeated over and over. *I will not kill Sherrie*.

It was Monday afternoon. After the exciting events of the weekend, the beginning of the new school week had been refreshingly uneventful. Kate had been glad to get back to the boring routine of classes. Her day had gone smoothly, with no surprises. She wanted to keep it that way. All she had to do was make it through one period with Sherrie and then she was home free. Derek Lowell had phoned Annie to say that he would be arriving that evening, and the girls had agreed to meet him at the hospital. But Kate could handle that. *It's all working out perfectly*, she thought happily as she entered the room.

Sherrie was already there. She had taken the trays of seeds—which had sprouted into tiny seedlings recently—out of their respective resting places and placed them on the table. When Kate walked up she was peering at them closely.

"Hey," Kate said, not friendly but not hostile. She was feeling pretty good about things, and she was determined that even being forced to work with her worst enemy was not going to spoil things for her.

"Oh," Sherrie said, "it's you." She gave Kate a cursory glance and went back to staring at the plants.

Kate gritted her teeth but didn't say anything nasty in response. "How are the plants?" she asked.

Sherrie looked up. "A lot better since I put the plant food in them."

"Excuse me?" Kate said, not sure she'd heard correctly.

"Plant food," Sherrie said again, as if talking to a child or a dog. "You know, food for plants? It makes them grow."

"You put plant food in the pots?" asked Kate, wanting to make sure she'd heard correctly.

"Yes," said Sherrie sharply. "So what?"

Kate slapped her forehead with her hand. "Sherrie," she said, "do you understand what this experiment is supposed to be about?"

Sherrie put her hands on her hips. "I'm not stupid," she said. "We're studying how plants grow."

Kate nodded. "Uh-huh," she said. "That's right. We're studying how plants grow—under very strict conditions!"

"Don't yell at me!" said Sherrie.

Kate felt herself getting madder and madder. She glared at Sherrie. "By putting plant food in the pots, you ruined the entire experiment," she said. "We were supposed to be studying the effects of water and sunlight on the growth of marigolds. Now, thanks to you, we'll have some very healthy plants but absolutely nothing we can use."

She was breathing hard and her heart was pounding. Sherrie just stood there, looking at her with a defiant expression on her face. She crossed her arms over her chest. "I don't see what the big deal is," she said.

That did it for Kate. She slammed her notebook on the table and picked up one of the trays of seeds. Turning it upside down, she dumped it on the table, dirt and all. It made a mess, scattering dirt everywhere.

"Hey!" Sherrie said, jumping back. "Watch it!"

"Why?" asked Kate. "Those plants were useless." She picked up the second tray and dumped it on the table as well. "So are those." She swept her arm over the remaining trays. "They're all useless, Sherrie. All those seeds—useless. All our data—useless."

"You should have told me," said Sherrie. "This is *your* fault."

Kate bit her lip. Her whole body was tense, and she could feel herself on the brink of losing control. How could Sherrie blame her stupid mistake on *her*? She was the one who not once but twice had ruined the experiment. The last time, Kate had been able to replant the seeds. But it was too late to do that again. They'd already lost a week's worth of data and time. There was no way they could catch up. Which meant that there was no way they could finish the experiment and get a passing grade. Thanks to Sherrie, she was probably going to fail the class.

She stared long and hard at the remaining two flats of seeds. Slowly she reached out, picked one up, and dumped it over Sherrie's head. Sherrie gave a shout and jumped back. As she danced around, trying to wipe the dirt out of her hair, Kate started to laugh.

"You think this is funny?" Sherrie asked her. "Let's see how you like it." She picked up the final tray and hurled it at Kate. The dirt went flying, spattering Kate's clothes and clinging to her in wet clumps.

Kate looked down at herself and then at Sherrie, who was still trying to wipe the dirt from her hair. Her face was streaked with soil, and she was looking at her hands in disgust as she tried to shake the dirt from them. Unfortunately for her, the only thing she had to wipe them on was the powder blue sweater she was wearing.

"That's it," said Kate. "You're dead." She flung herself at Sherrie and pulled her hair.

Sherrie screamed and slapped at Kate. She got

a chunk of Kate's hair in *her* hand, and the two of them stood there, yanking on one another's heads and screaming at each other. Each of them slapped at the other with dirty hands, leaving smears of dirt everywhere.

"You've had this coming for a long time," Kate said as she picked up a wad of dirt and ground it into Sherrie's face.

Sherrie spit the dirt out and tried to retaliate by grabbing some dirt from the counter and throwing it at Kate. But she missed, and accidentally turned on the water in the sink that was sunk into the tabletop. Water splashed out, turning the surrounding dirt to mud.

The two girls grappled with one another, each of them trying to get an advantage. Dirt and hands flew, and so did the insults.

"You and your stupid friends—" Sherrie began, but was cut off by a sharp pull on her hair.

"Think you're so—" Kate retorted, her words drowned out when she closed her mouth to avoid eating the dirt Sherrie was trying to hit her with.

The mud on the table soon became mud on the floor, and the girls slipped in it, falling down. They wrestled on the ground, getting dirtier and dirtier and madder and madder. Finally, Kate had Sherrie pinned and was thinking seriously about force-feeding her some marigold seedlings when she heard Ms. Ableman's angry voice.

"What is going on in here?" she asked.

Kate and Sherrie looked up at her. Then Kate looked at herself. She was a mess. Her hair, clothes, and skin were covered in mud. She was still holding on to Sherrie's hair. The floor looked like a mud pit, and the surrounding area wasn't much better.

"We had a little problem with our experiment," Kate said helplessly.

Ms. Ableman walked over and turned off the water, which was still running.

"Kate attacked me," Sherrie said, clearly faking sounding hurt.

"Kate, is that true?" asked the teacher.

Kate let go of Sherrie's hair. "Kind of," she said. "But it was because Sherrie ruined the experiment," she added hastily.

"I did *not*!" Sherrie retorted.

"Yes, you *did*!" said Kate, ready to start fighting all over again.

"That's enough," said Ms. Ableman sharply, making them both stop. "Now get up and go clean yourselves off. Then come back here and clean this place up." She turned to walk away, then stopped and looked back at them. "You both will receive Fs on your experiment," she informed them.

Kate got off Sherrie and stood up. Without a word she grabbed her notebook from the table and stormed out of the science lab, pushing the door so hard it banged into the wall outside. She stomped down the hall, not caring that people were staring at her openly as she passed by.

"Whoa, what happened to you?" asked Cooper as she and Annie, coming out of their classrooms, saw Kate and ran to catch up.

"Sherrie," said Kate shortly. "We had a little trouble with our experiment."

Annie and Cooper exchanged glances. Cooper bit her lip, trying not to laugh.

"Well," Annie said carefully, "that makes *two* of us who have gotten into it with her. First I slap her at Banana Republic and now you make her eat dirt." She looked at Cooper. "You're next," she said.

Kate laughed despite herself. It really *was* pretty funny, when she thought about it. Sure, she was probably going to fail science, but maybe seeing Sherrie all covered in dirt was worth it. Probably. Part of her was still horrified by what she'd done. But perhaps, if she explained, Ms. Ableman would let her do a makeup experiment.

She heard laughing behind them and turned to see Sherrie running through the hall. People were pointing and laughing at her, and she was yelling at them.

"Shut up!" she screeched. "Idiots!"

"Oh, yeah," Kate said to Annie and Cooper. "It was definitely worth it."

Kate had to go to the locker room and shower before she could do anything else. And she had to clean up the science lab as well. She told Annie and Cooper that she would meet them at the hospital when she was done.

Showered and dressed, she returned to the lab. Once again, Sherrie was already there. Unlike Kate, who always had a change of clothes in her gym locker, Sherrie had had to make do with cleaning herself off as best she could. That meant she still had streaks of dirt on her clothes. She didn't even look at Kate when she walked in; she just went on wiping up dirt and throwing the filthy paper towels she was using into a trash can.

Kate joined in silently. For the next half hour neither of them said a word to the other. They just cleaned. When they were done, and the lab looked pretty much as it had before their dirt battle, Sherrie stormed out, leaving Kate alone. Kate looked at the door separating the lab from Ms. Ableman's classroom. She knew she had to talk to her. As embarrassing as it might be, she had to explain why she'd done what she'd done. She took a deep breath and walked to the door.

An hour later Kate walked into the hospital. Cooper and Annie were sitting in the main waiting room. Kate walked over to them and plopped down in a chair. "He's not here yet?" she asked.

"He should be here any minute," answered Annie. "How'd things go back there?"

Kate sighed. "Well," she said, "you know how we're always talking about how the energy we send out comes back to us even stronger?"

Annie and Cooper nodded. Kate continued. "I'm living proof," she said. "I decided to give it to Sherrie, and now I'm getting it right back."

"No makeup project?" said Cooper.

"No makeup project," Kate replied. Then she grinned. "But it was still worth it."

They were all laughing when they looked up and saw a man standing in front of them. He was very tall and very muscular, with short-cropped brown hair, a worried face, and large hands that he was nervously taking in and out of his pockets.

"Is one of you Annie?" he asked.

Annie stood up. "You must be Derek," she said.

He took her hand and shook it firmly. Annie introduced Kate and Cooper as well. "Mallory is upstairs," she told Derek. "Sasha is with her, and so is Thea, Sasha's mother. She works a lot with runaway kids, and we thought it would be good for her to be here."

What Annie had said was only partly true. They *had* told Thea about contacting Derek, but only after the fact. While she'd been annoyed at them for doing it without consulting her, she'd agreed that it was probably the best thing to do. Still, she'd insisted on being there when he arrived, in case things didn't go well.

"We didn't tell Mallory you were coming," Cooper told him.

Derek nodded. "I'm not so sure she'll be all

that happy to see me," he said. "I was kind of the reason she ran away in the first place."

The girls all looked at one another. They'd been secretly worried that perhaps contacting Derek hadn't been the best idea they'd ever had. Now they thought maybe they'd been right.

"I was the one who raised her mostly," he said, as if they'd asked for an explanation. "Gram really couldn't do much, and since I was so much older than Mal, I kind of had to be her brother and her father. I guess maybe I was hard on her, but only because I love her. When I moved out and got married, it was just her and Gram. I couldn't keep an eye on her as much. When I found out she was getting into some trouble, I maybe over-reacted."

He stopped talking and put one big hand over his eyes. Annie cleared her throat. "It's okay," she said.

Derek wiped his eyes and sniffed. "I hope she'll see me," he said. "We all miss her so much. We've been so worried. Gram—" He stopped speaking again and took several deep breaths.

"Let's go upstairs," Cooper suggested.

The four of them took the elevator up and walked to Mallory's room. The security guard was still there, and he eyed Cooper warily as they approached. Kate stuck her head in, saw that Mallory was awake and seemingly alert, and said, "Hey there. We have a visitor for you."

Mallory gave Sasha a questioning look. Then Derek stepped into the room, with the girls behind him. When Mallory saw him, her face crumpled up and she started to cry.

Derek ran to her bed and put his arms around his sister. She put hers around his neck and hugged him, sobbing. Tears streamed down his face and onto the pillow while he repeated over and over, "I love you."

They stood, watching the reunion of brother and sister, until Thea stood up from the chair she'd been sitting in and said, "Come on. Let's leave them alone."

They all slipped out of the room and went to the end of the hall, where they stood talking.

"What happens now?" Kate asked Thea.

"The police will want a report," Thea said. "They'll have to check to make sure Derek is who he says he is. When that's done, they'll be free to go."

"Do you think Mallory will want to go with him?" Kate asked.

Sasha nodded. "She wants to go," she said confidently. She looked at her friends. "Most kids on the street want to go home," she said. "But most think they can't. Mallory may talk tough, but what she really wants is to be where people love her. Not out there," she added, nodding toward the street beyond the window they were standing beside.

Thea reached over and put an arm around

Sasha's shoulder. "I'm still a little mad at you all for keeping this a secret from me," she said. "But you did something really good here."

"All except for our ritual," Kate remarked.

"Ritual?" asked Thea.

"We did a ritual," Cooper explained. "To sort of teach Ray a lesson."

"But it didn't work," said Annie. "He still came back to try and hurt Mallory again."

Thea smiled slightly. "Tell me a little more about this ritual," she said.

They described the ritual to her, each of them adding details, until Thea had heard the whole story. When they were finished she shook her head, but not in anger. "It sounds like a great ritual," she said finally. "But maybe it wasn't the best idea you all ever had."

"Why?" Cooper asked. "We didn't ask for anything bad to happen to him. And believe me, he would have deserved it if we had."

"I know you didn't," said Thea. "But it was still motivated by revenge, wasn't it?"

The girls looked at one another. Finally, Annie shrugged her shoulders. "Maybe just a little bit," she said.

"The Law of Three is definitely true," Thea said. "But you can't go making the universe carry out justice when you think it's time. Sometimes, even when people deserve something, if you try to bring about what you think is the right end, you're the one who ends up getting hurt."

"Tell me about it," said Kate, thinking about the F she was getting in Ms. Ableman's class because she'd decided to teach Sherrie a lesson.

"But Ray *does* deserve to be punished," said Cooper, sounding frustrated. "It's not right that he's running around out there while Mallory is in a hospital bed."

"No," Thea said. "It's not right. But Ray is on his own path, just like Mallory is on hers and we're all on ours. You can't make him hurry along his path any more than anyone can make you hurry along yours." She paused. "However, that doesn't mean you can't do *something*."

"Oh, yeah?" asked Cooper. "What?

Thea smiled secretively. "Come on," she said. "We need to make a trip to the store."

CHAPTER 17

Sophia listened as the girls told her the whole story, starting with the break-in and ending with the arrival of Derek Lowell. Sasha did most of the talking, since in a way it was her story, but the others kept interrupting with details of their own.

"The stone," Kate said. "Don't forget the stone."

"Oh, and the Kali ritual," added Cooper at the appropriate time.

"Rover," Annie prompted. "Fido."

Eventually, after a couple of side trips, Sasha came to the end. She stopped talking and looked at Sophia, who nodded thoughtfully. "So that's why that bag of jewelry and money was waiting for me the other day," she said. "And here I thought the thief had had a change of heart."

The girls looked at one another nervously.

"There's a little bit of money missing," said Sasha. "Mallory bought some food. But I'll pay you back."

Sophia waved a hand at her. "That's the last thing I'm worried about," she said. "I'm just glad that she's okay. That *you're* okay," she added. "If there's any kind of trouble around, you guys sure seem to find it."

"Yeah," Cooper said, nodding. "We're pretty talented that way."

"Now, about this ritual you did," Sophia continued. "The Kali one?"

Again the girls looked anxiously at one another. Was Sophia going to scold them for doing a ritual they had no business doing?

"We thought—" Annie began, trying to head her off. But Sophia held up a hand to silence her. Annie stopped speaking and fidgeted with her braid.

"It sounds wonderful," Sophia said after a moment.

"Really?" said Kate.

"Really," replied Sophia. "I love the way you cast the circle, drawing on the power of fire. Elemental circles can be amazing tools of magic."

"That was my idea," Annie said brightly.

"And I love the idea of incorporating Kali into the ritual," Sophia continued, again making Annie smile happily.

"My idea, too," she said, earning friendly glares from the others.

"But," Sophia said.

Annie's happy smile faded.

"But?" she said.

"Thea was right," said Sophia. "As well-intentioned as the ritual was, it wasn't exactly kosher, if I may be allowed to mix my traditions for a moment. Asking a goddess to enact what you see as justice isn't something I recommend. Yes, it can work, but ultimately it's not the most positive use of your energies."

"But why?" asked Cooper. "That jerk really does deserve to get a good kick in the can."

Sophia and Thea laughed. "Yes, he does," said Sophia. "And it sounds like you gave him one. However—" She paused again, looking at them. "Who were you doing this ritual for?" she asked.

"For Mallory," Kate said instantly.

"Really?" asked Sophia, raising an eyebrow.

"Sure," Annie replied. "Who else would we be doing it for?"

"You've all seen news reports about death penalty cases, right?" said Sophia.

The girls nodded.

"Most of the time, the people being inter-viewed who are *for* the execution of a particular criminal say that they want to see it happen because they want to see justice for the victim, right?"

"Sure," Cooper replied. "They're angry that somebody killed one of their family members or friends or something. That makes sense."

"Yes," said Sophia. "Anger makes sense. But have you ever heard those same people interviewed *after* the execution? A huge percentage of them say that they actually *don't* feel any sense of justice, any sense of relief or closure."

"I don't get it," said Annie. "What does this have to do with our ritual?"

"Yeah," Kate said. "We weren't trying to kill anyone. We would never do that."

"I know," Sophia said. "I wasn't trying to equate the two things exactly. I was talking about what you hoped would happen as opposed to the reality of what happened. Your ritual was based on your love for Mallory. But it was also based on your anger at Ray. Energy raised out of anger can be very powerful, but it can also be very destructive, both to the target of that energy and to the originators of the energy. Much like those people who demand the so-called justice of the death penalty, you were doing something you truly believed was right, but it didn't have the outcome you wanted."

"Yeah," Cooper said defensively, "but just because Ray didn't get his. If he had, we'd be thrilled."

"No, we wouldn't," Kate said. The others looked at her, surprised by her statement. "Sophia's right," she said. "I didn't want to admit it before, because I really thought we were doing something that was right, but we were just doing what I did when I made Scott fall for me last year. We were trying to get results *we* wanted, not results that were necessarily right for Ray or Mallory."

Cooper sighed in exasperation. "But it *would* be good for him to be stopped."

"Maybe," said Sophia. "Maybe not."

"How can you say that?" asked Annie. "How could it be good for him *not* to get caught?"

"You're looking at this through the eyes of someone who cares about a friend," Sophia replied. "Do you remember when we talked in class about what it means when we don't get something we've asked for in a spell, like when we do magic to help a sick person and that person gets worse, or even dies?"

Annie nodded. "It's not because the spell didn't work," she said. "It's because the person's path needed to take her in a different direction."

"That's right," Sophia said. "It's always okay to *ask* for something, but we have to accept when what we've asked for isn't what the universe thinks we need."

"Okay," Cooper said. "I get that maybe we tried to force something to happen that we didn't have a right to force. Maybe we stretched the whole 'and it harm none' thing a little. But what *should* we have done?"

"That's why we're here," Thea said. She turned to Sophia. "I thought maybe we could show them how to adapt the ritual they came up with a little bit."

"I think maybe that could be arranged," said Sophia. She looked at the girls. "Do you remember everything you said and did?"

Annie nodded. "I remember my parts."

"I remember the Kali invocation," Kate replied.

"And I remember the chant," Cooper added.

"Good," said Sophia. "Write down the words. We'll go set up the circle."

As Sasha, Thea, and Sophia prepared the back room for the ritual, the three girls wrote out the words of their ritual. It didn't take long, and after five minutes, when Sophia came back to check on them, they were done.

"Thanks," she said, taking the papers. "Let Thea and me look at these for a few minutes. You guys go get ready."

They walked into the back room, where a circle of candles was waiting for them. Sasha was already seated inside the circle, her hands in her lap and her eyes closed.

"Sophia said I should meditate and imagine that I'm sitting in a ring of fire," she said.

The others joined her, sitting across from one another so that they were at the four compass points of the circle. They all sat quietly, waiting for Thea and Sophia.

About ten minutes later, Sophia and Thea entered the room and stepped inside the circle with the girls. Thea was holding a drum, and Sophia a cauldron, which she placed in the center, just as the girls had done. Then Sophia motioned for them to stand up, which they did. She stepped outside the ring of candles and, as Annie had done in the original ritual, picked up a candle and began walking around the circle.

"One time 'round I cast the circle with the fire of protection," she said, using Annie's words. "May this circle be a place of safety and refuge. Two times 'round I cast the circle with the fire of change. May this circle be a place of cleansing and renewal," she continued, changing Annie's original wording slightly. "Three times 'round I cast the circle with the fire of truth. May this circle be a place of healing and understanding."

She returned to the circle. "We are in the circle of fire," she said. "Here all illusion is stripped away and we stand surrounded by the cleansing flames of truth. The circle is powered by our desire for renewal and change."

Sophia raised her hands and closed her eyes. "Into this circle of fire we invite you, Mother Kali. You who sweep clean the illusions of the world so that we may see it anew. You who devour the darkness and give birth to stars. Be with us here. Help us in our magic."

When she was done she motioned for everyone to sit down. Then she leaned forward, struck a match, and dropped it into the cauldron, which sprang to life with fire. The girls had seen this particular trick before, and knew that the cauldron contained a little bit of rubbing alcohol, which burned brightly without smoking.

"Kali does indeed bring justice," Sophia said as the flames snapped and popped. "But more important, she clears the paths. She rids them of obstacles and illusions that might hinder our journeys. Tonight we are asking her to do that, both for Mallory and for Ray. We might not understand Ray's path, but that is not our job," she added, noting the bewildered looks on the faces of the girls.

"Look into the cauldron," Sophia instructed them. "As we chant, imagine the fire in Kali's cauldron burning away the illusions that prevent us from seeing things as they really are. Imagine it lighting the way, showing us a path that before lay shrouded in darkness."

Thea began to drum. After a moment, she began to chant.

> In the belly of the cauldron,
> in this circle made of flame,
> call we up the burning power,
> conjure it in Kali's name.
>
> Burn away the old illusions,
> show us what is true and right.
> Set our feet upon the pathway,
> lead us through the dark of night.
>
> Crackling, sparking, never fading,
> fire pure and fire wild,
> go and do our magic bidding,
> light the way for Mother's child.

The girls sang with her, the words old and new at the same time. "Picture Kali walking ahead of us," Sophia told them. "She is carrying her cauldron, and the light of it shows us the way. Others walk beside us, behind us. Mallory and Ray. Maybe they stay on our path, or maybe they turn to follow other paths, following their own fires. It doesn't matter. What matters is that we are all walking, seeing one step at a time."

They sang the chant through perhaps a dozen times while Thea drummed. Then her drumming slowed and their voices faded out. As Thea tapped out a steady, simple beat, Sophia spoke some more.

"There is danger in the darkness," she said. "But Mother Kali's fire protects us as long as we remain on the path. We don't fear the shadows or the strange sounds. We know that the fire in her cauldron shows us the truth. We know, too, that those who don't follow truth she will deal with in her own way. But that is for her to decide."

She stopped talking and just let Thea drum. Each of the girls, listening, was lost in her own image of Kali, and of the path she revealed to them. When the drumming finally stopped, they all looked around at one another.

"Wow," said Cooper. "That was intense."

"It's amazing," Annie said. "It was a lot like our original ritual, but those few changes made it completely different. I feel relaxed and peaceful now, where before I felt all worked up."

"Your ritual was beautiful," Sophia said. "This is just a different way of harnessing that same energy. This time you turned the energy inward instead of directing it at Ray. You empowered *yourselves* instead of giving it away."

"I still don't like him, though," Cooper admitted.

"You don't have to," said Sophia. "I don't like him, either. But don't let your hatred of Ray take away from your own power. Leave him to his own path while you walk yours. I guarantee you, he'll get what's coming to him when it's time. It's when we try to change things before it's time for them to change that we become frustrated. Now, let's join hands."

The six of them linked hands. "We're going to open the circle now," Sophia said. "But I want to do it a little differently. I want you each to imagine taking some of the fire into yourselves. I don't care how you do it. Drink it like water. Breathe it in. Let it soak through your skin. But take some of the fire—some of Kali's fire—into yourselves."

There was silence as each of them imagined taking the fire into her body in her own way. Then Sophia intoned, "The circle is open but unbroken. Carry it with you. Let it fuel you and light your way. Let it bind us together like a golden chain."

They all squeezed hands and then let go. The ritual was over.

"We should get back to the hospital," Sasha said as they cleaned up. "Derek and Mallory will probably be wondering what happened to us."

They said good-night to Sophia and got back in Thea's car. As they drove to the hospital, they talked about the ritual they'd just done.

"There's something that's been bothering me a little," Annie said. "I understand that magic doesn't always work the way we want it to or the way we expect it to. But if we always say that it's because maybe things are supposed to go another way, isn't that just an excuse for it not working? I mean, how do we know if magic is real at all if when it doesn't work we say, 'Well, that's what was supposed to happen'?"

"Good point," said Thea. "You could very well ask the same question about people who pray for something to happen and get the opposite result. Does that mean that prayer doesn't work or that God doesn't exist?"

"I think it's a matter of why you're praying or why you're doing the magic," said Kate after a moment. "It's like Sophia said—if you're doing those things to try to change something because *you* want it to be changed, that doesn't necessarily mean that the change you want is the thing that needs to happen. Sure, it seems to make sense that praying for someone not to die is the best thing. But maybe it isn't."

"Okay," Cooper said. "But then what's the point of doing magic at all if the thing that's supposed to happen is going to happen anyway? Why not just say that everything that happens is what's supposed to happen and there's nothing you can do about it?"

Nobody spoke for a long time. Then Sasha said, "I do think everything happens for a reason. But I think, too, that it's up to us how to use what happens in the most productive way possible. I mean, it would be easy for me to look at what has happened to me in my life and just say, 'Clearly, I'm supposed to be on the streets getting into trouble, so I might as well just get used to it because there's nothing I can do about it.' But I didn't do that. I tried to change things. I *did* change things. I took the path with the light ahead of me instead of staying in the darkness."

"I think that's what this year has really been about," Annie said. "Doing magic is only a small part of Wicca—and of life. What we're really learning is how to use our gifts to make every opportunity and challenge we're given make us stronger people."

Cooper sighed. "This all sounds great," she said. "And I agree. So why do I still want someone to crack Ray over the head?"

They all laughed. "No one ever said this stuff was easy," Thea reminded her.

They arrived at the hospital, parked, and went inside. When they exited the elevator at the fourth floor, they were surprised to see a police officer standing by the nurses' station.

"Oh, no," said Sasha.

They ran down the hall toward Mallory's room, where they saw a police officer positioned outside the closed door. The girls tried to go into the room but were stopped by the cop.

"Where do you think you're going?" she asked.

"Our friend—" said Sasha.

"We have—" Cooper added adamantly.

"But—" Kate and Annie said.

The door opened and Detective Stern looked out. "What's all this noise?" he asked irritably. Then he saw the girls. "Oh," he said. "It's you."

"What's wrong?" Cooper asked. "Why are all these cops here?"

Detective Stern opened the door. "Come on in," he said.

The girls rushed in. When they saw Mallory sitting up, happily talking to Derek, they breathed a collective sigh of relief.

"What's the big deal?" Sasha demanded.

Detective Stern nodded at Mallory. "I was just telling Miss Lowell and her brother the good news," he said.

"Good news?" Cooper asked suspiciously.

"We caught that Ray fellow," the detective said. "About an hour ago. Picked him up trying to buy a gun at a pawnshop downtown."

The girls all looked at one another. "You're sure it's him?" asked Cooper.

Detective Stern gave her a sharp look. "Would you please have *some* faith in me?" he said. "I know you're the big crime fighter and all, but give me a little credit, okay?"

Cooper grinned. "I'll give you more than that," she said. She went over and gave the detective a hug. "Thanks," she said.

"Turns out this guy has warrants out for his arrest all over the place," the detective told them when Cooper let go. "He's not going anywhere for a long, long time."

"We are, though," Mallory said from the bed.

Everyone turned to look at her.

"We're going home," she said, looking at her brother, who took her hand and held it tightly. "As soon as they say I can leave."

"I can't thank you all enough for what you've done," Derek said to the girls. "If it wasn't for you, I don't know what might have happened."

"Yeah, well, it all works out the way it's supposed to, right?" said Cooper, grinning at her friends.

Later, after saying good-night to Mallory and Detective Stern, the girls headed for home. As they walked out of the hospital, Annie said, "Well, one more challenge met and conquered."

"Two," Cooper said, thinking about her mother.

"Yeah, but what's next?" asked Kate.

"For me it's going to be meeting my sister next month," said Annie. "Mardi Gras, here I come."

"Lucky you," Kate remarked. "I'd love to go to New Orleans."

"Me, too," said Cooper. "I'd love to see all that voodoo stuff."

"And see the parade," Sasha commented.

There was silence for a moment. Then Kate said slowly, "You know, we *do* all have a week off from school."

They stopped and looked at one another.

"But this is your trip," Kate said to Annie.

Annie nodded. "Uh-huh," she said. "But Juliet says she has *lots* of room."

They all looked at one another for a long moment before Cooper said, "Girls, I think I feel a road trip coming on."

with book 14:
the challenge box

Kate stood up and walked to the box. At first she wasn't sure how she was supposed to get anything out of it, as there was no discernible lid and there didn't seem to be any way of opening it. For a moment she panicked, thinking that maybe *this* was the test and she was failing it. Then she noticed that the center of the box's top panel was actually a circle of black velvet, and not wood. She poked at it with her finger and discovered that there was a slit in the velvet. She pushed her hand through and into the box.

Just as Sophia had promised, the box was filled with slips of paper. Touching them with her fingers, Kate was reminded once more of the dedication ceremony and how she'd hesitated before selecting the slip of paper with her word on it. That time she'd been terrified about what accepting the challenge meant for her life. Now she was afraid again, but for a different reason. This time she knew what accepting the challenge meant, but part of her was terrified that she might not be able to meet it. Then what would happen? If she wasn't accepted for initiation, she would have gone through a lot of trouble for nothing.

She pushed her fears away, knowing that thinking about them wasn't going to help. One thing she'd learned about magic was that you had to meet it head-on. Before she could second-guess herself any more, she grabbed a slip of paper and pulled it out. She looked at it, then looked at Sophia.

"Do I tell everyone what it is?" she asked.

"No," answered Sophia. "You should show me and Archer, because we need to know so that we can see how well you accomplish your challenge. Other than that, I recommend keeping your challenges to yourselves."

Kate looked at her paper again, then showed it to Sophia and Archer. Archer, who was holding a notebook, wrote down Kate's challenge. When she was done she nodded at Kate. "Good luck," she said.

Kate returned to her seat, the slip of paper clutched in her hand. She thought about what was written on her paper. Would she be able to do it? She hoped so. But she wasn't sure. She looked at Cooper and Annie, who were seated beside her, watching the proceedings. She very much wanted to discuss her challenge with her friends, to see what they made of the task she'd been assigned. But

Sophia had told them not to. It was going to be up to her, and her alone, to figure out exactly what the words on her slip of paper meant. For the moment all she could do was watch as the others went forward to reach into the Challenge Box.

Annie was the second of the threesome to go forward. She reached in and felt around. She stirred the slips of paper with her hand, hoping that some feeling—some sign—would come to her when she touched the right one. But there were no flashes of light, no trumpet blasts or voices telling her to pick a particular slip.

You're overanalyzing this, she told herself. *That scientific brain of yours is working overtime. Just go with what you feel.*

She closed her eyes, stirred some more, grabbed a handful of slips, and then let all of them but one fall from her fingers. The one that remained behind she pulled out. She showed it to Archer and Sophia before she even looked at it herself. After she'd read it, she folded it carefully and tucked it into her pocket as she returned to her seat.

Cooper waited an unusually long time before standing up and walking to the Challenge Box. But unlike Kate and Annie, once she was standing in front of it she didn't hesitate at all. She plunged her hand in, snatched up the first slip she touched, and pulled it out. She read it, an indecipherable expression passing over her face as she did so, and then presented it to Sophia and Archer to be recorded in the book. Then she walked back to her friends and sat down.

The three friends sat and waited for the other class participants to finish choosing their challenges. None of them said anything to the others, but it was clear that they were all thinking about their own challenges. When the last person had drawn a slip from the box, Archer closed her notebook and Sophia put the black cover over the Challenge Box once more.

"Now you have your challenges," Sophia said. "You have two weeks to complete them. We won't have class next week, and will meet again on the fourteenth of March. At that time you will each be expected to give a short description of your challenge and how you did—or did not—complete it."

"That's it?" asked Cooper, sounding surprised.

"You expected more?" asked Sophia, laughing.

"Well, yeah," Cooper said. "This is the last class, right?"